Exploding mind

There's lots of pain

From circuits cut and pieces left behind

That's how you go insane

All disconnected.

SHRIEK

an absurd novel

Davide A. Cottone

Legal Deposit Lodgement: (In accordance with the Copyright Act 1968)
National Library of Australia
State Library of Queensland
Parliamentary Library (Qld)

Cataloguing-in-Publication Data
National Library of Australia
Author: Cottone, Davide A., 1947 -
Title: Shriek
ISBN: 978-0-9925293-3-8
Notes: An absurd novel. Fiction.

Cover created by AllyOop Designs www.allyoopdesign.com.
Created by Kues 1 – Freepick.com (Right Face)
Created by Asierromero – Freepick.com (Middle Face)
Book production by Carolyn Martinez –
editor@hawkeyepublishing.com.au
Editing: Paul Vander Loos: paul.vanderloos@gmail.com

DEDICATION

This book is dedicated to those people who are deemed 'unfit' to impose their will, their thoughts or their very presence on a pristine, polished, conformist society. In that society, the 'moderately unfit' are pensioned off and condemned to become fringe-dwellers devoid of hope or rehabilitation, and put on a steady diet of television, drugs and alcohol.

Those who persist are 'quarantined' in institutions and sedated with medication or whatever other means considered necessary. Stereotyped as being 'up there with the fairies' or 'in la la land', the novel, as well as the following poem, are proffered in their defence.

Lament from La La Land

Reality
Is the norm
Accepted, indisputable, irrevocable, inviolable
And perpetuated in perpetuity
By a closed mind.
La la land
Is quite absurd
They fence it off to keep those inside in
Who hear too much or see too much
Say too much or think too much
And to keep those outside out
Who accept 'the norm'
And must not be corrupted.
So, here's to *La La Land* and all its member states.

ACKNOWLEDGMENTS

A heartfelt thank you to my advisers and 'beta' readers: Elizabeth, Laurel, Claire, Tonino, Jenni, Dr Michael Wilson, Debbie Terranova, Carolyn Martinez and Paul Vander Loos for their suggestions and corrections.

My special thanks also go to my highly intelligent friend Lyle Kerswell for his advice and consent to reproduce a part of his life's story which adds authenticity to this tale celebrating *difference* in society.

AUTHOR'S NOTE

This is a socio-political novel partly written in the absurd genre. Although some events may ring true for many of you, it is a work of fiction.

It addresses three major pressure points impacting individuals and places in our 21st century world. Firstly, it attempts to address issues of mental health that are endemic in society. Secondly, it is set in a world where there is a clear and present disconnect between the real and the virtual. Finally, it reveals a proliferation of dysfunctional governments and how their control over people has infected the ways of that world.

In many cases, religion has been the catalyst. It is suggested that religion as a tool for absolute power through a divine right may now be vying with *the love of money* as *the root of all evil.*

Umbugumbuland is everyman's country where the events in this story predicate the future. The brutality of war, the tools of technology, and the breakdown of our humanity have desensitised individuals and created a new norm. Blood and bone have nourished the seeds that have flourished with the rise and rise of dissident and militant groups. This produces a genetically altered new-world order that is the crop the world now reaps and feeds upon to sustain it. Must we fear for the future or a past which is unable to accommodate it?

PROLOGUE

I ask myself, who would ever believe that Aleph McNaught's view of the world was once just blood on his knuckles? Nobody – because he had another name at the time.

It was only in his early twenties that he changed his name to Aleph McNaught after his second stint in mental rehab. By that time, he had already learned that blood on the knuckles was not the way to a better life.

Aleph had a lot of snakes to handle after experiencing a horrific childhood of mental and physical abuse. He was going to make it no matter what so he had to ensure his previous persona was dead and vaporised. The change of name was so successful that he developed a passion for personas.

That's the way it was with him – he had this capacity to conjure up mindsets which provided a vehicle for him to cope with his shortcomings and disappointments and satisfied his needs in a clinically controlled manner.

I also ask myself, why would anybody want to make up place names like Umbugumbuland and all those other places when there are so many real places to choose from? That's absurd.

Because he's not just anybody, Aleph sees himself

as someone who doesn't want to be carrying any baggage other than his own in his quest to make the world a better place. His ideas are his and his alone. They do not derive from any culture, prejudice, stereotypes, places or countries in the reader's world. Any similarities to persons, places, events or countries are purely coincidental.

I'm giving you the heads up on Aleph. He's simply trying to make a point, that's all. He wants to tilt the axis of the old world order just enough to make a difference to the way people think. Only then can the megalomania of politics, economics, society and religion cause the old world order to spin out and unravel. In its place, a new world order will gather up the threads on an axis realigned to the demands of an ever evolving 21st century world of chaos, virtual reality, artificial intelligence, crypto currencies, cloud computing, high frequency stock trading, high frequency terror threats, catastrophic climate change fallout, mind bending with false memories and fake news, mental illnesses like post traumatic stress disorder and drug-induced psychosis, and whatever other pet hate humanity may have in store for us.

I don't want you to give up on Aleph when the going gets tough. I don't want you spitting the dummy before you realise who the real dummy is.

For Aleph, only the absurd is real.

CHAPTER 1

Hello, it's me Aleph. I see you've been given the 'heads-up' on me. That sort of thing pisses me right off sometimes. I can speak for myself, you know. This is *my* story.

On many occasions in this life, I have found myself being tossed about and rolled over by an anger tsunami because I didn't have the means to compete, the gall to exploit others, the nerve to take advantage of a situation, or the sense of self-worth to eyeball an adversary. I am angry with myself because those inadequacies amount to one word – a scab called *failure.*

Time can commence the healing. When the crustacean auto-ejects, it reveals a crimson underbelly, delicate to the touch for days, months or even years until the colour fades. A maturing scar remains, which is the everlasting mark that *failure*, like a branding iron, sizzles onto your psyche.

When I've had enough and there's simply nothing more that I can take, I go up a gear from a scream to something turbocharged that can summon the chanting priests of penance to perform the miracles that can put a stop to all the pain. Like a whistling kettle, I must go an octave higher, from a whistle to something shrill to gain the attention I so desperately need. Sex and hallucinatory drugs work for me, as do the shamans operating on the shadows in my mind. Always on call as well are the sorcerers of science and medicine. They have all the answers to every syndrome, disease, complaint, complex or condition. They issue their decrees for medicinal drugs, surgery or detention for those they deem demented.

So many things can catapult me into that somersault where I lose control to inertia. Brutality, hatred, ridicule, torment, bullying, disappointment, betrayal and unrequited love all do it to me. I crash, and when the sparks from my brain-fry die down, only darkness remains. That's when the next round of pain and suffering incessantly pummels the nerve endings of low self-esteem, self-hatred and depression into a frayed and dangling mess, causing the onset of what I call *psychoplegia* – a state varying between partial and complete paralysis of the psyche.

You don't want to go there. It's like swimming in a bucket of vomit. It's a cave where you go to hide surrounded by walls and a ceiling that are forever closing in on you as you revert to a Neanderthal crouch and try to reassure yourself that you are still alive so that you can keep on fighting. I cut myself and I bleed to confirm that I'm still alive. Some people bang their heads against a wall. Others burn themselves, or carve words or symbols on the skin, or pierce themselves or pull out their hair. Those who don't understand, call it self-harm. Those who do understand call it necessary; the safety valve in the pressure cooker that releases the steam and stops your brain from exploding.

There's a recurring flashback that probably has some bearing on why I am the way I am – that is, if you can believe what Freud or Jung found when they went out digging for psychoplegia roots to feed to the pigs. You can make up your own mind about it because when it comes to shrinks, I lost faith in them a long time ago.

Anyhow, I am sitting in my room reflecting, as much as a sensitive seven-year-old Christian kid is capable, on the gravity of my misdemeanours. Shivering and totally abandoned to my fate, I accept that I am guilty of contravening God's laws, being ungrateful for all my blessings and disrespectful of my parents' public standing among all the other parishioners of our church. What is worse is the fact that ours was a fundamentalist religion with grassroots faith based on the word of God and only the word of God.

'You're a miscreant!' a menacing figure hovering over me shouts.

It's my stepdad Jack. He always used big words, even at church meetings, so people could admire him as more of a man of God.

Whack!

'You're an ingrate!'

Whack! Whack!

'You have no respect for your parents!'

Whack! Whack! Whack!

I see the shine of the leather razor strap as it bears down on me. It had been made smooth like a mirror of dull brown glass from the daily rub of the cold steel of his cut-throat razor. The flip-flap of steel on leather was not unlike the flip-flap of leather on my thin skin.

'Hopefully, this strap will sharpen your perception of our concern for you. Spare the rod and spoil the child. Never a truer word spoken … after all, it is the word of God.'

Whack! Whack! Whack! Whack!

I am again abandoned to my misery, left with the welts rising all over my body. I wondered why he needed to use the strap when I already accepted that what I did was wrong. I should not have skipped Sunday school. I had never done it before. A firm reprimand would have been enough to ensure I would not do it again. But Jack believed I deserved that beating. Every time I did something wrong, he insisted I deserved the beating. There was no learning curve. Learning was spontaneous once you had been exposed to the word of God. It was either learn and remember or face His wrath.

His words of chastisement have echoed back and

forth in my mind to this day. It made me want to curl up in the corner of the room and shield myself from the strap swishing in the wind and the pain that permeated tender skin to nerve endings that relayed it on to my brain.

However, the worst was yet to come. The door opened to this evil-eyed man determined to finish the job. He began punching me, making me buckle under the weight of each blow, and it only ended when I lost consciousness.

'Think of this punishment as medicine. It will make you better,' he said.

Once I pass out, the respite is that I can't feel anything anymore. Bit tragic hey? In fact, whenever I felt unwell, depressed or desperate enough to end it all, I provoked him until he beat me unconscious again. That's self-harm and that's what I call tragic!

You probably think I'm a bit of a looney talking like this, but people at school who should know, assessed me in a far more positive light.

'He's off the charts when it comes to the measurement of his intelligence.' This was what my counsellor once wrote to my doctor who read the comment to my case worker in front of me. The case worker then passed the information on to Jack who reminded me of it the next time he beat me. Great relay team I had behind me – the counsellor, doctor, case worker and Jack. There were no gold medal hopes in that lot.

'And that's exactly your problem; you get too big for your boots and you need to be cut back to size,' Jack told me.

So, although those beatings continued year after year after year until I became a teenager, I had discovered an open wound in Jack's thick skin and was learning fast how to rub hard up against it. The intelligence thing really bugged him, especially when he began losing arguments with me. All I could rely on to hold my own was his ultimate weapon of choice against me – the Holy Bible. At 16, I could quote large passages from the Bible verbatim, and every time he struck me, I would use God's words in retaliation so he could never justify his cruelty towards me. 'Strong in the head and weak in the flesh' was his only justification after each beating. The niche wound kept festering and my persistence was probably what drove him to drink, but drink only caused him to beat me harder with anything he could lay his hands on.

Where did my mother stand while all this was going on? She did nothing. I was happy with that because I was worried that if she interfered, Jack might beat her as well. I could never have survived that mongrel hurting her. She was everything to me and he knew it. In fact, he was jealous of me as the only other male in her life that wasn't a ring-in like he was.

I made sure I kept reminding him that he was nothing to her. It was like sticking a knife into that poxy wound of his. It was worth the recriminations.

Ultimately, he knew he was the real loser because he didn't have the DNA to refute the fact.

The neighbours certainly didn't care. They knew but they just laughed along with Jack as they swilled down their beers together. They belonged to the same religion as we did and were always patting him on the back because he was so eloquent and knowledgeable, especially on church matters. No-one was game to take on Jack. Whether it was at church, work, home or in the community, Jack exuded a confidence that he possessed a divine right to his authority on all matters and over everyone, all attributed to his firm religious convictions.

Everybody probably thought that it wasn't very bright of me to provoke him the way I did, but intelligence was more than just being bright, it was about having an innate sense of right and wrong and a conscience. Jack had none of that. He was a bigot and a hypocrite. He had other women and flaunted it when he drank with his mates. He was a tormentor and an arsehole who leaned heavily on the older folk in the congregation to contribute money they could not afford to the church's coffers. Try explaining any of that to him in biblical terms. I tried on two occasions, and he hospitalised me.

Jack agreed, perhaps foolishly, to me taking martial arts lessons after I turned 16. He knew the martial arts were all about respect, taught the importance of discipline, and championed proper behaviour. He probably figured it would get me off his back as he couldn't abide the way I prodded him all the time.

Jack justified the cost of tuition to my mother by telling her, 'At least they might be able to teach him something about respect, discipline and how to behave.' However, if he thought that was the reason I wanted to learn, then it should convince any sensible person that he really was not that bright.

I showed my masters the respect they deserved, and they rewarded my behaviour and dedication with special attention in improving my technique and self-confidence. Within 12 months I was top of my class. I practised every waking hour until I had worked my way up through the ranks and eventually mastered the prerequisites needed for my black belt. On the day before I turned 17, I was pronounced ready.

I never did gain that black belt. Instead, I fronted up to Jack and sat him down on his arse with a few swift well executed moves. Then, when he got up again, I laid him out flat on his back before he even had time to cross himself. All the hairs on my body seemed to rise up as if to catch that wave of ecstasy that had been so long in coming. I was hyped up on adrenaline, and after the second round, he no longer got up, and the ambulance had to be called to take him to hospital.

My last words to him were 'You need to learn respect, discipline and how to behave, you bloody hypocrite'. I felt good. I was a man at last.

CHAPTER 2

After I had finished that chapter with Jack, I found myself in a *'déjà vu of kangaroo tail stew'*. For the uninitiated, a *'déjà vu of kangaroo tail stew'* is a stew made from the tail of an old man kangaroo. Sometimes it can be so tough that it must be boiled several times before there is any hint of the meat coming away from the bone. You eventually come to recognise the same bone in a different stew after so many stews.

The result of my assault on Jack was that I was hauled out of the house, crammed into a police van and dumped into the lock-up at the local cop shop. I reflected on the gravity of breaking the law, which was something that had become the story of my life, and hence the *'déjà vu of kangaroo tail stew'*.

My contemplation was cut short when I was shunted into an office and stood up before the police sergeant, 'Tom the Toad'. An equally burly but obese and sweaty constable, nicknamed 'Tweetie' because he was always whispering threats into the ears of detainees, had already summarily convicted me.

'The actions of this boy are beyond the pale, sergeant,' he blasted in my ear.

He picked up a huge paddle that was hanging on the wall behind him, shoved me towards the sergeant, and struck me across the buttocks.

Whack!

My whole body was thrust forward and my face ended up only centimetres from the Toad.

'It beggars belief that 'e would assault 'is own father. Fairly sat 'im down on 'is arse, sarge, and laid 'im out flat on his back 'e did.'

Whack! Whack!

I swerved to one side to avoid smacking into the Toad as my face almost ended up in the top drawer of his desk.

'Get him out of here. You know what he needs,' Tom the Toad said.

The constable replaced the paddle on the hook on the wall and substituted it with one of those heavy rubber truncheons that can break your bones without leaving a bruise. He hauled me back to the lock-up where he made it clear to me what he thought about how I had treated Jack.

'Boot camp; that's what they need to sort out blokes like you. Just like they 'ad in the old country.' The truncheon came down with a resounding thud.

'This little dolly can do the job just as well.' He hammered my body with blow after blow.

Whack! Whack! Whack!

I knew it would soon be over as I screamed upon reaching my threshold of pain. Another octave up and I passed out. Halfway through to the point of blackout, as I lay on the floor of the cell, I could feel the boot occasionally being sunk into my abdomen.

I woke up to find myself on a filthy mattress on the floor. It stank of vomit which was probably mine. I wondered why the constable had to use a paddle, a rubber truncheon and his boot to convince an intelligent person like me that my actions were against the law. I decided to tell him how I felt about this when he returned to check if I was still alive.

'Surely officer, there must be a more civil way to go about all this than the paddle, a rubber truncheon and the boot. Even with your fucking use of cockney, I would have had little difficulty getting the message.'

He stomped in the cell like a wild bull on a rampage, and knocked me to the ground. I could feel both horns lodge deeply under my ribs and lift me off the floor. I could see the bloodshot rage in his eyes and the saliva dripping from the corners of his mouth as he dropped me and began trampling me with his hoofs. He leaned back long enough to put his size 14 boot on my head, effectively trapping me.

'I'll tell you what your problem is, laddie. You're too fucking smart for your own good.'

That's when I vomited again all over those size 14 boots; it was the last I saw of him.

I avoided fronting court because my English literature teacher presented himself at the police station early the next morning. He told Tom the Toad that if I wasn't out of the lock-up and back at school by lunchtime, he was going to come back with the local MP and a few journalists from the city who were itching for the sort of scoop this whole sordid event would provide. I was crouched in the corner of my cell but heard it all. It was like an angel calling out from Heaven.

My English teacher was pretty switched on. I wished I could pull a bluff the way he did. It was only because he was an out-of-towner that he could get away with it. Nobody in our town could ever put it over Tom the Toad and his *deputy dog* Tweetie.

The sergeant himself came in and gave me a towel and pointed me towards the shower. I was out of there before I could call him 'Tom the Toad' to his face. Just kidding, I'm nowhere near that dumb. It was tempting though. Maybe I'll do it next time.

I returned to school to a hero's welcome because everyone knew what Jack was like and they all thought he deserved it. But back home it was a different scenario. Jack had piled up my things outside the front door as he had already decided to throw me out of the house. The few possessions he let me take included some old clothes, my school books, and my guitar which he had busted. What broke my heart was watching my mother looking old and worn out, shifting the curtains at the window to gain a last glimpse of me as I left. That glimpse was worth a thousand words to me. It expressed her love, sorrow, despair and helplessness. Another scar on my psyche. I didn't care what happened to me. I would happily carry the suffering of the world on my shoulders as long as she was free of it. How would she fare when I was gone? I vowed I would take him out for good if he hurt her.

'This isn't a threat, mongrel, it's a promise,' I shouted from outside the house. 'If I so much as hear a rumour that you have hurt my mother when I'm gone, I'll come back in the middle of the night, drag you out of bed and stomp on your head until you're dead.'

I walked down the road and sat on the bench at the school bus stop. It was there that I imagined I was Shakespeare's Hamlet at the lowest point in his estimation of his self-worth:

What a piece of work is a man!
How noble in reason, how infinite in faculty!
In form and moving how express and admirable!
In action how like an Angel!
In apprehension how like a god!
The beauty of the world!
The paragon of animals!
And yet to me, what is this quintessence of dust?

The only change I made to the whole soliloquy

was that I substituted the word *dust* with *shit.* That was exactly how I felt.

Fortunately, I didn't have to sleep out on the street that night. My English teacher, Mr Thomas, found me at the bus stop and asked the principal for permission to put me up overnight at his place. I was smoking a cigarette that someone must have just lit up and discarded when their bus came because it was almost full length. He didn't ask me to put it out.

'Come on, hop in. You can stay with Pam and me tonight and then we can sort out all your needs tomorrow morning. You'll love Pam, she's a social worker and she has got more contacts then there are hairs on a chook's bum.'

'I thought there were supposed to be feathers on a chooks bum,' I queried.

'I wouldn't know but you are about to find out because we're having chook tonight and you're going to be the one plucking it.'

His down-to-earth nature was all I needed to put me at ease. The recent trauma started draining out of me, and for a moment I thought I had pissed myself. However, it was a relief of a different kind that meant someone who could really make a difference actually cared about me.

I plucked the chook that night, and Pam stuffed it and placed it in the oven with potatoes, pumpkin, onion, sweet potato, and herbs and spices that she claimed were from a secret recipe that her grandfather had brought from overseas.

Pam later asked me to tell her my whole story, which started her crying. I felt bad that I had brought sadness into her house, and apologised.

'Please don't apologise,' she begged. 'These are tears of happiness,' she insisted as she wiped her eyes.

I was pleased about that but had my doubts when she started sobbing.

'I'm just so happy that we have been given the opportunity to give something back after all the good fortune we have had in our lives. Mr Thomas tells me you have excelled in your studies of English and that you can recite more of Shakespeare's soliloquies than he can. Who knows what the future will hold for someone like you once you are given a chance?'

That certainly was a boost to my self-confidence, but I had been there before. Things always turned out like multicoloured soap bubbles that blink at you as they vanish, leaving you wondering what happened.

'I don't know, Mrs Thomas. Sometimes I think I will never know happiness. I figure it's because I never knew my father. I missed out on a lot of the things that other young boys had. They could share things with their fathers. Young boys need their fathers ... or at least an uncle or a granddad. All I've ever known is that anti-Christ of a stepfather Jack. He's stuffed with my head. I'm damaged goods.'

I turned to Mr Thomas. 'You know what I mean, Mr Thomas. Hamlet the crown prince had the world at his feet. He could have married the beautiful Ophelia and lived happily ever after. His life was destined to end tragically and I fear the same for me. You see, the life inside my head is always going to be different from the life I lead. It has a life of its own; a memory. Even good fortune and great success can't erase a memory.'

'Well, we'll see about that. We want you to know that we're here for you,' Pam said. 'That's not going to change.'

Well it did. The next day she organised for someone in social services in the city to set me up in a boarding house near the school for the rest of the year so I could finish my high school education. I'm sure they would have been there for me if Mr Thomas hadn't been transferred to a school out west. I reckon it was a conspiracy by Jack and Tom the Toad to kick away the crutch the Thomases had afforded me.

All that fucking with my head was beginning to get to me. My social worker made a request that I be prescribed Valium, which was supposed to relieve *the anxiousness that results from the gap between the expectations of a fulfilling life and the realities of a stifling existence.* It wasn't meant to dumb me down so I couldn't blame the medication. What it did do was take away my motivation. All I wanted to do was float and I soon found the perfect answer to that. Another down-and-outer at the boarding house gave me a taste of what he called 'an angel peeing on your tongue'. It wasn't really anything special. It was just plain old marijuana, not buds or anything like that. In fact, I reckoned he used to mix it with dried banana leaves to make it go further. Anyhow, it gave me what I wanted, which was to escape from the real world without the big leap into oblivion. I was prepared to try anything that would remove the memories of my childhood. I trusted both my doctor and my housemate because both their treatments made me feel better and both were preferable to the 'feel better' treatments Jack had dished out to me. At least I graduated despite having spat the dummy several times in those final months. Somehow, I managed to stuff it back in without choking, and struggle on.

The one good thing that came out of all this was that my mother walked out on Jack. It was just after I graduated. She joked that she had a new job as a housekeeper. After the divorce, she got to keep the house! I don't know where she got that one but it certainly wasn't her, she had no sense of humour.

My first priority was to earn some money. I took on a job as an apprentice mechanic at a service centre near where my mother lived, and moved in with her. I liked the work, and the study was elementary compared to what was the usual for me. The money, freedom and the part-resurrection of my self-esteem opened a whole new perspective on life. It was as if metal clamps had been removed from around my head to allow me to look to the left, right, turn around and make choices and decisions for myself instead of bowing to the will of others. I could imagine another life where I was no longer the black sheep who only did bad things and was the embodiment of shame and embarrassment.

People at work were good to me. There was never any talk about me being too big for my boots, a troublemaker or a smartarse. They sat and ate their food with me. The only other people who did this before were my lookalikes who lined up with me at the school tuckshop early in the mornings before school. We looked alike because we all had shared similar experiences the night before – beaten up, thrown out of the house, and hungry. A small group of ladies at the tuckshop always came early to feed us just after 6am so we would not lose face in front of the other children who labelled us as *'povvoes'*. We would follow-up with a shower, and exchange our uniforms from the previous day with a washed and ironed set from their stores. Those ladies were our childhood angels, our guardians, and our life support.

However, I had tasted the nectar of the netherworld – Valium, weed, alcohol, party drugs and eventually the hallucinogenic drugs like DMT and LSD. I was forever drifting in and out of the world of work which I loved and the other world where the tools of trade just floated by, forever out of reach and useless to me. My drug-wedded friends were always there to offer my outstretched hands another fix or assurance that I was doing what I had to do to live life to the full. I needed to experience how it felt to be carefree, having a sense of wonder, knowing safety, kindness, comfort, trust and friendship. I had missed out on this as a child and it was all there on a platter for me, waiting to be consumed in one form or another.

Then to complicate things further, I fell in love.

Let me just tell you one thing – when all you know is hate, it is almost impossible to be loved or to fall in love. Call me a sucker, but this love animal doesn't come with a bridle. There's nowhere you can attach reins to maintain some control over where it takes you. Like a mug, I just jumped on bareback and held on to whatever I could. Nothing I did or said made any sense. Prepare for some surprises!

CHAPTER 3

I figure that at this point in the story of my life, you probably think I've been dealt some lousy cards apart from the falling in love bit. Consequently, unless you're heartless, you are wishing for my impending wedding to that true love so that I will live happily ever after. Well, let me assure you of one thing so you don't go to bed disappointed – that is not going to happen.

Apart from knowing that I fell in love and that it was a deep, heart-crippling and soul-exorcising love, I could not remember anything else because I had deliberately blanked out everything to do with that love affair. It was the only way I had of surviving the continuing nightmare it had become. In fact, the only thing I recall of the relationship I had with Penny Black is what I recorded after I was detained in the mental health ward of the general hospital in Cannabia, the capital city of Umbugumbuland.

Before I go any further, I want you to know that from here on, I'm giving false names to all the places, including countries, because I don't want your existence or your reality to make you feel you're a part of this. I know some people have a propensity to be offended the moment their intellect is challenged, or they feel unable to cope with people who have a tragic story to share. This story is about my existence and my reality; it's blood and bone stuff, not *Alice in Wonderland*. You are welcome to come into my world, but know that it will always be vastly different from yours. Unless you are mad.

That's right, as I wouldn't wish it on anybody, I'm deliberately locking your world out. Therefore, you can always opt out and pretend that whatever you heard never really happened. Umbugumbuland can be relegated to *'mumbo jumbo land'* and you can go back to whatever you were doing. That's what people often do in this world, it's a matter of survival. You're no good to anyone dead, or mad. I don't expect you to take me too seriously but I do want you to hear my story. It's not everyman's story but it has been on the periphery for centuries. Now is the time.

As Salvador Dali once said:

There is only one difference between a madman and me.
The madman thinks he is sane.
I know I am mad.

Well, anyone who could paint something like *The Great Masturbator* and get away with it obviously had a point to make. That's all I want to do – make a point. This book is *My Great Masturbator*.

The girl's name was Penny but I referred to her as Penny Black. The main reason was that the *penny black* was the first adhesive postage stamp ever printed. That alone made it special, and Penny Black was special to me. She was my first only true love.

My behaviour throughout that whole period with Penny Black was so bad that it was no wonder I was arrested. It was so extraordinary that I was transferred to the mental health facility for assessment by a psychiatrist. I could have been committed to a mental institution. In fact, I firmly believe, society might have missed out on its one real chance to put me away forever. The only thing that might have saved me from a lifetime among *crazies* was my thorough knowledge of the Bible. It added the wisdom to every answer I gave to every question regarding whether I understood what I had done and whether I deserved a second chance.

I don't like to blow my own trumpet but that psychiatrist was impressed, and I mean shake-your-head-in-disbelief impressed. He gave me a clean bill of mental health, and explained my bizarre behaviour as '*a temporary foray into the inexplicable, brought on by a drug and alcohol induced psychosis*'. He added, '*This lad exhibits higher levels of thinking that go beyond point of view, analysis and conclusion and into the metaphysical.*

At the very least, he is outstanding in his knowledge of the Bible and exhibits a capacity of memory that might be attributed to savant syndrome'.

That statement got me out of there when I probably didn't deserve a second chance. If you can believe the backstory to it all – which I can't bear to read because it is so not me – I should have been stamped *'Never to be Released'.*

You've had a glimpse of my world Part One with Jack, and if you think that was bad, welcome to my netherworld Part Two. You need to read the statement, although it might become tiresome or depressing at times.

Introducing yours truly – the one, the lonely, the morally and physically dishevelled, terror-struck, conflicted, withdrawn, contemptuous, hostile, scornful, scathing, repugnant, paranoid, irrational, degraded, mortified, suicidal and broken loser. That was me. How a man of my intelligence could become so devoid of faculty, crass and undeserving of life on this planet much less deserve a second chance 'beggars belief' as Tweetie would have reminded me.

Here it is; my statement compiled after the event with Penny Black. The year was 1966.

I'm nineteen years old and it's a bit hard to remember now as I stand here in the washroom adjacent to my room in Ward 9C. I'll take it one step at a time. I'm here as an inpatient for a mental health disorder assessment which the court imposed on me over some pretty bad behaviour prior to my recent arrest. My mind is cleansing itself of toxins. I'm not sure if the toxins are a result of the drugs or the girl or a mock-up combo of both in a kumquat sauce, which is how I imagined them.

This much I remember: I was a second-year apprentice mechanic. It was a Friday. I had two weeks' holiday and was quite keen to get home to start them. I picked up my mate Fred after work and was giving my 1962 SV1 Valiant a flogging when I crashed it opposite the cop shop into the fire station. After a quick inspection of the damage, I wanted to get the fuck out of there. The Wog Chariot was a bit hard to drive with one front wheel labouring as it ground against the inside of the mudguard. We got home and three hours later I had it stripped down fully. I was glad to see all the damage was repairable. Fred and I threw on some Stones' music, got totally stoned and ripped into my home brew. That part's clear.

Next morning, I woke up and couldn't remember anything about the night before so I started smoking my bong that I had specially packed before I crashed the car. Baz turned up, so I woke Fred who was still asleep on my lounge and we had a session and a bit of a strap of my guitars then decided to hit the city early to get pissed. We were keen to check out a new club called 'Rip and Snort'.

We hung out at the West Bank Pub, then the Victory. Fred had to go home, then Baz and I walked into the 'Rip and Snort'. It was a bit freaky at first, with some weird looking dudes dressed in black with face paint on playing pool. I got myself a beer and asked the music DJ dude to play the Stones' recently released 'Paint It Black'. We played doubles with the freaks. It was my shot when two chicks walked in dressed like death. They sat near our table and both hauntingly stared at me. I was wearing my light blue jeans and blue flanno.

I had very long hair back then and these girls were trouble. I remember telling myself that no way would I go for either one of them so I had another drink. Meanwhile, one of the freaky dudes was chatting to them and he came up to me and said the girls wanted my name. I looked and one of them wasn't such a bad sort, kind of Mediterranean. Anyway, she got up and walked past me so I accidently on purpose hit her in the crotch with the back of my cue while taking my shot. She smiled the smile and I knew I was in.

She came back from the loo and I had a drink waiting for her. We got to talking and I forgot about my pool game. Her eyes were burning. It was time to take her home. Baz gave the cabby directions while I had my face full of tits.

The funny thing was it was only about 6.30 when we got back to my mum's place. I was very happy to find out my mum wasn't home. Well we didn't stuff around. The 'fred' was on and I still had her warmed up ready. A fair bit later, mum gets home from the club. She saw Baz and asked after my whereabouts. He told her I was in my room but warned her not to go in because I had a chick in there.

So, mum comes storming in ... well what do you do? Five minutes later we came out clothed and mum kicked me out. I guess she was sick of all the loud music and drug taking and outright disrespect from me. Anyway, I rang my step-brother Jimmy who had come over the previous weekend and offered me a room at his place, so it was a good time to take him up on the offer. He picked us up and we moved in over there.

Penny was 18 and up on holiday from Cannabia for a week staying at her friend Rina's place. I walked her to the train station and thought that would be the last of her. With Penny gone and back to being alone, I was off the drugs and alcohol and chilling out just fixing my car and tossing a lot of other things over and over in my mind.

I figured I was on a road to nowhere. Life keeps throwing situations at me and I find myself predictable. I still see my life as simplistic. I worry that I'll die and leave nothing behind.

Anyhow, back to Penny ... I nicknamed her Penny Black. If only she hadn't remembered my address and sent me a letter ... bummer. In her letter, she gave me her number. I was keen for more sex so I called, and the next thing I know I'm off to my dealer to score for her. Penny Black and Rina had been tripping the night before and they were still a bit trippy. I didn't really like either one of them, and when I found out Penny Black's boyfriend

Michael had chased her up from Cannabia and was on his way over, I knew it was time to leave. They were trying to talk me into beating him up for them. Apparently, he was Rina's boyfriend before Penny had stolen him off her. I decided to bail.

The next day Penny Black rang and wanted to see me so I was back over at Rina's place to see her while Rina was at uni. Penny had fully broken up with Michael the previous night and he and Gina had got it on. That day I asked Penny Black to be my girlfriend. She said 'yes' of course. She said she had to go back to Cannabia to tell her parents she was moving to Hoopla up north to stay with some dude she had met on holiday. That sort of thing was difficult to say over the phone.

So, I had a new girlfriend. I can remember being a bit worried about Penny's moral values right from the start, but she promised she wouldn't screw anybody else while she was with me. The next day was market day and we all went and I scored some acid for us all. It's funny how strange things happen when you're on acid. Two days later she returned to Cannabia for two weeks.

Over that time, I had become good friends with Rina. We had hung out with each other on a few occasions and I learned a lot about Penny Black that I was probably better off not knowing. For instance, on the night I met them, they were having a competition on who could get the guy and I was the guy. They were even on how many guys they had slept with and I had become Penny Black's number 9. What kind of sluts' game is *that? But not to be outdone, Rina screwed both the evil dudes and got to 10.*

Two weeks passed and I was back at work. Rina was madly in love with my older step-brother. Rina and I went to Wolla Street bus station to meet Penny who was returning from Cannabia. I knew instantly she had slept with somebody because I felt sick. It really put a downer on my excitement at having a new girl. I grabbed her bags, loaded the Chariot, and took Penny to Phil and Audrey's place. They were friends of Rina's and she would be staying with them. We smoked some pot that she had brought up from Cannabia then went to bed. She felt cramps from her bus trip so I gave her a massage. My intuition was still bothering me re Penny Black's faithfulness, so I asked if she had cheated on me while she was away. She said 'no' and we made love. Afterwards we went upstairs to smoke with Phil and Audrey and Rina. They had 'northern lights' and we got very stoned. I kept seeing everybody as evolved monkeys.

In the morning, I woke up crying for some unknown reason. I became disorientated. Penny Black had got some magic mushrooms from the Cannabia Botanic Gardens, so Baz, Penny, Rina and I decided to go camping. We headed off to 'Lost World', my favourite camping spot. It was my first mushy trip but something bizarre happened that night. We experienced a group hallucination of thousands of back to back rainbows. Nobody mentioned them at the time but the next day we all started describing the same picture.

After the mushrooms wore off enough, we headed back to Hoopla. Penny moved in with me. Everything was pretty cool. My weed was harvested and we were all happy for a while.

We got a dog and called him Brutus. We went to concerts, nightclubs, a wedding and we went shopping a lot. I got sacked because the workshop went broke. My boss Grant found me another job but I quit it after two hours because my new boss had given me the shits and I caught him looking at my arse. That day Baz, Penny Black and Rina had gone to a hemp rally. I went into the city and found them. They were quite surprised to see me.

So, as it turned out, we were both on the dole and it was good – the sex, my weed and my friends. I spent a lot of time with her and we did everything together. Sometimes, Rina would come around and she and Penny would reminisce about the good times in Cannabia, which irked me because they kept referring to their slut's game and I grew to hate her. Something plagued me in the back of my mind. We started to argue. It was mostly me. I hated her but I loved her. I was obsessed with her and it was slowly driving me insane. I started taking Es and Ts by myself and drinking a lot. I started slashing up my wrists then going to palm readers to see what they would say. I crashed the Val twice more and got the shits living with Jimmy so we moved back into my mum's. I got a job at Fiveways Fixers Garage which was only five minutes' walk from my mum's place.

One night Rina put me out of my misery and told

me that Penny had cheated on me with two blokes while she was in Cannabia, just so she could be ahead of Rina at their sluts' game. It was a relief to finally know the truth after six months of knowing inside my gut that something was wrong.

I confronted Penny and she finally admitted it. My heart broke because I loved her. I slashed a vein in front of her. I think if she had told me the truth in the beginning, I would not have reacted so badly and would have got over it soon enough. However, as it turned out, it felt like broken glass shredding every cell in my body as the fragments ripped through my veins.

We took off to Cannabia the next day because I wanted to beat the fuck out of Luke who was one of the guys she fucked. She was pretty cool with it. I cried the whole way on the bus trip down. I was messed up with a broken heart. Only God knows what the other passengers thought of me on the bus.

We arrived at Penny Black's mum's place. Her parents seemed nice enough for unemployed dope smokers. I finally understood something about her upbringing. As for Luke, well I couldn't find him because he had been tipped off, so we decided to return to Hoopla.

After that, Penny Black and Rina weren't friends for a while. I had developed some jealousy and trust problems and our relationship was going downhill fast. I cut my hair short and had a big hit of acid and speed, enough to put myself into a psychosis. I couldn't sleep. I was awake for 20 days. My brain was running in overdrive and on empty in terms of reasoning. In brief moments of clarity, I would find myself standing at the flea market in nothing but my boxer shorts, walking the streets with the street signs constantly changing, holding a flower and watching it die slowly, my name being called out from bushes in a friendly growling voice. I had visions of Jesus laughing at me ... me jumping out of a car doing 60 ... praying to God or trying to poke out my right eye. I had put all the stones in their place. All my sins were coming back to haunt me.

I had lost it, yet for the first time in my life I was free. I had become enlightened somehow but everything and everyone reminded me of the pain in my heart. I destroyed nearly everything in my room. That's when Penny Black left me. I got some pot so I could bring myself down and she came back when I had snapped out of it about a month later. After that, I was forever different towards her. I started treating her like absolute shit. I was willing to keep her but I would make her pay. A few months later she ran off with Michael back to Cannabia, so I screwed Rina and moved out of mum's place.

I moved in with a school mate, Shane. My hair grew long again. I spent my time hotting up the old Wog Chariot. It fucking flew and I loved it. But nothing I did could fill the Penny void, so I wrote a poem and mailed it to the slut. She came running back. I guess I have a way with words. All my life I've felt alone. I felt like moving away from the people I knew, so we decided to live in Cannabia. I applied for a job soon after we arrived, and got it easily.

They paid me good money and things were great, but when we applied for rental accommodation, we kept on being rejected. It was probably because we looked like a young hippy couple on drugs. I was sick of living at Penny Black's parent's place as I felt uncomfortable.

A year went by and things were good. My plants were in bud and I had made some new friends. Then things got shitty. My dog Brutus broke into a chicken coop and killed all the chickens. Then someone stole my plants, all except for one 9 foot 'northern lights' and all of Penny's plants. Then I noticed Penny was flirting with her friend's boyfriend and my friend from work. I had had enough. I thought 'fuck it all', quit my job and went back to Penny's parents' place and started packing.

I was angry and turned up the music till it was real loud. Penny Black's dad opened the door to the room and asked me to turn it down; he wanted to talk to me. I told him to fuck off. As he started to walk into the room, I picked up a box of fireworks and a lighter and told him to fuck off again. He then tackled me onto the bed and pulled my pants down. I yelled out to Penny Black's sister to call the police. I punched him in the head several times but it had no effect, so I palm-heeled him in the nose then tiger-clawed his nose half off. Blood was everywhere. He got off me and held his nose. I then jumped through the fly screen out the window into a rose bush. I was fully stuck.

The next thing the police showed up. They were more interested in the marijuana plants then me stuck in the rose bush. They called an ambulance to take me to hospital. I walked into the hospital and waited, and in the meanwhile pulled all the rose thorns out myself. I hitched a ride home and just got my car keys and wallet and got out of there.

I left all my belongings and drove for about 40 minutes before I ran out of petrol. I grabbed the jerry can and hitched a ride to the next servo, filled it up and went in to pay. And what do you know, there's no money in my wallet. At this point I cracked. I started yelling and screaming and then started walking north. It was cold. I walked for miles and found a blanket on the road in front of me. I wrapped it around myself and kept walking. The road started to veer east so I left the road and walked through the hills until I found myself blocked by a swamp. I had no choice but to walk through it. It stank and I was wet and freezing.

The sun had started to rise and I took off my clothes and hung them on a fence to dry, and walked to the top of a hill. I found a waterhole and jumped in to wash myself despite the cold. I sat on a big rock and waited for the sun to warm me up. Hours passed and I went looking for my clothes but couldn't find them. I started following the fence line thinking that I would find a farmhouse. There were sheep everywhere and they started bahing. It sounded like they were saying 'Mooooooses … Mooossses'. When they started saying 'Jeeeesus … Jeeesus', I knew that I was starting to lose it again. It was probably from walking all night and a bit of a flashback from the mushrooms I had the previous week.

I eventually came upon a farmhouse where I was faced with the dilemma of being naked. I looked for a clothesline but there were no clothes on it. I went behind the shed where I found a welded iron box. I held it around my waist and went to the house and knocked on the door. They answered and I politely asked for some clothes. They were a nice old couple. They invited me in out of the cold and told me their son had recently moved out and had left some clothes behind. I got dressed in some blue jeans and a nice shirt. They made me a cup of tea and I asked to use their phone but they didn't have one. They told me to follow the phone lines until I found a house where the line was connected. I was keen to get my situation sorted out, so I headed off.

I came upon a house where the phone lines were connected, and knocked on the door. A woman came to the door and freaked out. I asked if I could use her phone and she said 'no' so I asked her if she could ring someone for me. She rang someone but it was the cops. She told them I had a knife … fucking lying bitch! She also called a neighbour who quickly showed up in a ute. I asked him if he could give me a lift to the nearest town and he obliged. We were driving along when we came upon a police roadblock where the police apprehended me and searched me for a knife. They took me back to the police station in Udder where I told them the whole story. They were amazed as it was minus 6 degrees the previous night.

They rang my boss in Cannabia and he told them I was a good bloke who had some problems with his girlfriend. The police gave me a bus ticket and a food voucher. I had some breakfast and then waited for the bus back to Cannabia.

When I got off the bus, I walked to Penny Black's house where they let me in but refused to give me my money. They said they would drive me to the airport and put me on a plane, so what could I do? All I wanted was to get my money and my car. They drove me to the airport where I went mental at them and refused to get on the plane. Because I was going off, the security personnel at the airport said they would not let me on the plane anyway, so we got back in the car and they drove me to the hospital where they told them they thought I was mental. I thought, 'Well, I'll have a chat to a psych and they will see that I'm not insane and let me go get my car'.

When the hospital insisted they wanted to keep me in for a few days, I went off and said, 'No fucking way!' and tried to leave. Six blokes from their crisis team confronted me and tried to restrain me. I fought them off but they got a mattress and forced me against a wall. They injected me in the backside and I was out.

I woke in a cold cell and was trying to reflect on what had happened. I saw there was no way out but suicide. I bit into a vein on my arm which gushed out blood. I then got the sheet off the mattress and tied it to my wrists and wrapped the sheet around my neck. I stretched my arms out tight until I could not breathe, and the weight of my arms held the sheet tight. I blacked out.

I woke in darkness crying. I was terrified. I heard voices telling me to shut up, that they were trying to sleep. I couldn't see anything and I could not stop crying. Voices from nowhere tormented me. I felt my soul diminish to the point where it was almost gone. Then it vanished in a flash of light and the voices were gone. I felt whole.

When I awoke, the blood had been cleaned up, my arm was bandaged and there were no sheets on the mattress. Finally, the cell door opened and two guards escorted me out. We walked down a corridor of cells and came to some doors without handles. I had lagged a bit but they were not worried as there was nowhere for me to go. I noticed a fire hose cabinet and tried to open it but it was locked. I harnessed all my strength. I forced the handle and opened it and got the hose and turned it on as the guards were signalling the nurses in the office to open the electric doors. There was a half door to the office where the nurses were, so I blasted the guards then turned it onto the nurses who fled the office. I jumped the half door into the office and went through a door into a courtyard where there was a corner wall with two downpipes. I started to climb when a nurse grabbed my leg. I kicked her in the head and she let go. I made it to the roof and to the edge of the building and jumped to the ground, spraining my ankle.

I limped onto the road where a car pulled up. The dudes in the car had seen it all. They were laughing and told me to get in. They said they had just got their methadone from across the road. They had seen me on the roof and knew it was a loony bin. They drove me to the city.

I didn't know where to go or what to do next. I walked around until I saw a group of blacks in a park. They said I could stay there with them if I had nowhere to go. So, I stayed with them for two days then decided to go back to Penny Black's place to get my money.

I got to the front door when the police arrived and handcuffed me and took me back to the loony bin. I realised there was no escape, that I needed to go through the system. Well they drugged me up big time. It was like a lobotomy. They made me face a tribunal where it was stated that I had caused grievous bodily harm and something about burning an effigy.

I was sentenced to serve 35 days in the mental ward pending a full assessment. I can tell you, I was distraught. I had done nothing wrong.

Welcome to my alter ego. I'm a cunning porcupine. I know me and I don't talk like that. That statement was a methodical, monotonous, stream of consciousness piece of verbal diarrhoea that was crying out for exoneration on the basis that I was out of control, young, in love and under the influence of drugs. The object was to elicit the desired response from the shrink who was sucked in by a shit story that might not even have happened. Nobody checked out any of it. These guys with all their education were so naive; it was as if they had never left school. They were soft pussies with puppy-fat blubber for brains.

I, on the other hand, was thick-skinned from being beaten up, neglected and hated, and from having to wait in line on most school days for breakfast with other bottom-feeders. That conditioning made me both brittle and resilient and taught me to prey on the conscience of softies like Pam Thomas. She fell for my tale of misfortune and was desperate for the 'opportunity to give something back after all the good fortune they had in their lives'.

Welfare workers and tuckshop ladies are the same. If you can get them emotionally involved, they become a pushover for us pros who are always on the lookout to reclaim some of the benefits from a system that has failed us all our lives. Shrinks are even easier because they already have a term, like 'induced psychosis' or 'savant syndrome', that academia has invented to give authenticity and a rationale for their diagnostic decisions.

Don't get me wrong. I like people like Pam Thomas and welfare workers and tuckshop ladies. Thank

God for people like that and for shrinks and priests who aren't paedophiles, and all the other do-gooders out there. If you can get them on side, they can certainly use their positions in society to your advantage.

As you are about to find out, if you don't keep your wits about you, you could end up more in a state of confusion than enlightenment. I know, because I have already written this book once and passed it around family, friends and professionals like lawyers, teachers, shrinks, street loungers and bums, and you wouldn't believe how many of them missed the message and lost the plot, especially when it comes to the ending which is supposed to reveal the identity of the cadaver in the coffin.

I wouldn't wish that on anybody, so I've dumbed it down a bit. No offence intended, but I'm even more aware of it after writing that first draft of the book.

To be fair, you should know what happened to me after I was released. I became a peaceful, intelligent, God-fearing man … on a pension! They figured I might be intelligent, I might be God-fearing, but my behaviour was not rational and my condition at best was fragile as in *handle with care*. I was slotted into the category of one-percenters who simply had difficulty fitting into civilised society.

All the psychologists and social workers assured me they understood my problem. Even the police began to accept that beating me up was probably not the answer, even though that course of action usually worked well in the past. As for being law abiding, it depended on the benchmarks you set for defining good, bad, right and wrong. I couldn't understand why they kept referring to it as 'my problem'.

My condition in this life was a prison. I could never be relieved of it because I had been pigeon-holed for life as a misfit in society. The mould was flawed from the start and nothing could be done about it except deny it, break it, and to keep it out of the public eye because it represented failure of both the system and those who perpetuated it.

At the age of twenty-one, I was the typical black sheep – an odd phrase chosen to epitomise worthlessness. I felt worthless and I was drowning in my own vomit.

CHAPTER 4

You might as well hear from me now, because you are about to find out that I'm an important character in this story, and I want you to get the gist of it from every perspective. I'm Yeahwellah.

You see, Aleph, the protagonist, tends to skew everything in his favour. It's his way or out-of-the-way with that guy. At times, he comes across as quite conceited, yet at other times this guy can melt your heart. He can be an outright shit one day, and next day he can offer you his last potato chip. When he's on a downer, he doesn't hit the mat; this guy ends up under the floorboards.

At twenty-one, I have no doubt. I'm the black sheep. I feel worthless and I'm drowning.

Those are the words he said to me, but don't underestimate his capacity for survival. He's the sort of person who won't stop until he is totally and permanently mentally and physically incapacitated. When his tyres are flat, he runs on the rims, and when they fall apart, he burrows underground to pop up where you least expect him.

One day, at the Hoopla Hospital Mental Adjustment Facility down in 'Ward War 1' as he named it, Aleph pulled off a real ripper of a manoeuvre that stunned a lot of people on both sides of the notional normality line that differentiated greater mortals (the community at large that needs protection) from lesser mortals (the community within that needs detention). At the time, Aleph's mind must have been floating off on its way to another planet, and he decided to anchor himself to earth by throwing a heavy cast-iron chair through the glass viewing panel that staff used to monitor inmates in the communal recreation area.

I was also in 'Ward War 1' at the time. What originally brought him to my attention was the fact that he stuttered. Having been afflicted with a similar problem since my early childhood, I could identify with the frustration that day that caused him to snap.

I found out all about the beatings he took as a child and how religion wrought havoc on his mind, and I heard about his tragic love affair with Penny Black. They certainly were considerations that needed to be weighed carefully when it came to understanding a guy like Aleph. He had become bitter and he needed to rediscover his faith in God during this period of inner turmoil that was choking him. Even though I can be a bit over the top sometimes with my religious fervour, I felt I could help him rebalance, so I offered to be there for him. He, of course, turned the problem back on to me which was so typical of his style. He suggested it was I who needed help and he offered to be there for me. Either way, in the beginning, we were good for each other and were the best tag team ever.

Aleph also had a habit of naming people, and Penny Black was a case in point. Her name was Penny but he called her Penny Black because the Penny Black was the first stamp that had adhesive on the back which he claimed caused him to 'get stuck' on her.

He did the same to me. Here I was talking to this guy, who at times had an indecipherable stutter, yet he had the hide to call me *Yeahwellah Welliwasgonnasay* because I had a slight stutter. I reckon someone probably called him that as a kid and he wanted to palm it onto someone else. I could hear him chuckling to himself every time he called me that. Maybe it was because I had difficulty handling my disability and that gave him some sort of perverse joy.

Nevertheless, it was worth persevering with the friendship despite his idiosyncratic shortcomings. He had a distinct flair for understanding and engaging other people and taking them into his confidence. Still, with Aleph, you could never feel comfortable in his presence because he played mind games to rules that could be quite chaotic, illogical and even absurd at times. Put simply, what you saw or heard was not always what you got with Aleph, so you had to be stoic because that's the way he operated.

We certainly had a lot in common and we hit it off from the beginning. I'm like him; one minute I can be this loyal friend and support person, and in the next people want to rip off my head or beat me up. He could be fully engaged and enjoying my presence, and in the next breath accusing me of being too close, or as he puts it, 'never further than a dog's piss away'. If that isn't tantrum talk, I'd like to know what is.

I thought you should know this.

CHAPTER 5

I'm in here again and on Valium, the ubiquitous prescription drug of the time, after another relapse of my Penny Black induced nightmares. The good thing is that my thoughts are flowing again although there is a lot of staccato in the messages being relayed to my brain. When I say *'in here'*, I'm not talking about one of those places where you have a hot cup of coffee beside you and you're curled up with your partner opposite a warm fire watching a feel-good movie and eating popcorn.

'In here' for me is being up to my tits in the stench of the trenches of Ward War 1. It's a ward that they invent a new name for every few years to fool the rest of the population into thinking that loony bins no longer exist.

This time I've beaten them at their own game and named it myself. I mean, how could anyone give a place like this the name they have plastered out the front of the building – Hoopla Hospital Mental Adjustment Facility. What the fuck are they supposed to be adjusting? Is it the carburettor that causes my brain to be starved of fuel for rational thought? Is it the tappets that hammer at my brain like a mechanical typewriter? Is it the braking problem that never seems to pull me up in time to keep me out of trouble or the hand brake that won't release when I want to get going again? Is it the fan belt that's so tight it makes me squeal or so loose that I keep overheating and blowing gaskets? Is it the sound from my muffler; like do I fart too loudly when I'm asleep? Hey! I'm a mechanic. What do you expect?

'In here' they curl you up in a straitjacket or strap you to the bed and give you electrotherapy. That's why I needed to find a way to get out. If I had to spend time in that ward, I didn't want to suffer the indignity of being treated as a nutcase or the trauma of living with what was going on in the minds of many of the inmates.

I found a solid iron chair, which at the most opportune moment, I picked up and tossed through the massive viewing pane that staff used to monitor what was happening in the courtyard communal area. If you're the typical shriek-seeker who loves watching other people do weird things you always wanted to do yourself, but not be held responsible for the outcome, then this little sideshow act is for you.

Well, it was as if I had just lobbed a beehive into the ward, as staff and inmates ran amok, colliding and tripping over one another, arms, legs, hands and wrists gyrating to an imaginary island dance routine. The only way of telling the difference between both groups was that the inmates were all wide-eyed, aroused from their drug-induced stupor, while the staff were all like zombies in solidified shock. I don't know what happened after that, because security overpowered me and jabbed me with a pacifier. But I do remember what happened when I came to. It was exactly what I had planned.

After that display of defiance without so much as a bleat from this little lost sheep, everyone treated me with caution and the respect I deserved. The inmates thought I was dangerous or at best unfriendly, and the staff thought it was better to appease me, give me whatever I asked for, and look for any excuse to get me released as soon as possible. I was classified as a VIP as in 'very irritable person'.

To help pass the time, I delved into mind games with the psych staff, toyed with the support staff, and fostered an allegiance built on mutual trust and respect with security. Consequently, I was left alone most of the time without too many constraints placed upon me. In fact, they rewarded my model behaviour by letting me out of the ward for specific periods of time.

As for my fellow inmates, building that relationship took up 90 per cent of my time. For those that I classified as misfits, it was important to get their confidence and trust. I empathised with their plight. I shared their distrust and sense of betrayal by anyone who had in any way conspired to put them there in the first place. They felt they were being victimised because they were different and misunderstood. I genuinely did feel for each one of them.

The ones I categorised as genuine 'crazies' needed personalised attention. Often these guys try to control you, and if they succeed you become their bitch. They take over your psyche while you are in their presence and remain there as a major influence on your behaviour unless you wrestle back that control. Often that can be really hard to do.

A case in point was Yeahwellah Welliwasgonnasay. I called him that because he had a bad stutter and would preface every statement with the words 'Yeah … well … ah … well … I was gonna say'. The only problem was that sometimes he had to utter those words several times before he got out what he actually wanted to say. That can get under your skin and play paralysis games with your psyche.

Yeahwellah went about the ward all day imitating Jesus. He wanted to save the world but nobody wanted to be saved. I explained how Jesus had the same problem in so many ways. Eventually, I convinced him that maybe he had been chosen as a sort of conduit for doing God's work. He was pleased about that, and when I began quoting slabs of scripture from the Bible, he wanted to know if it was he who was inspiring me. I assured him I felt inspired in his presence and convinced him that maybe Yeahwellah was a variation of *Yahweh*, a

Hebrew form of the name for God in the Bible. Maybe his stutter was simply his way of speaking in God's name, or because he was in some early stage of beginning to speak in tongues. That's how I cracked him. He never left my side after that. He was never more than a dog's piss away but sometimes it became a bit uncomfortable when you were the lamppost. Mum would have understood that one.

Sometimes I'm not quite sure who is who and what is what. Yeahwellah was a shadow; my shadow. He had no form, no feeling, only movement. He moved only when I moved. Otherwise, he didn't exist. Go figure.

To get the attention I needed to reinstate my case before the medical supervisors at the ward, I decided to pursue the savant syndrome that had been alluded to in that report from the psych after the Cannabia episode. If I could convince them I had savant syndrome, my freedom (with benefits, I might add) was assured, because savant syndrome was not recognised as a mental disorder. That was where I drew the line; the moment I allowed them enough cause to declare me as mentally unstable, then that would be the moment this little black sheep would surely drown.

There was a huge flat-black chalkboard and a box of chalk in the courtyard where many of the inmates wandered aimlessly, or curled up in corners or simply sitting muttering to themselves. As I took up a piece of chalk, Yeahwellah lurked in my peripheral vision holding a wet cloth for me in case I needed to erase or rephrase anything as I set about my task.

I began transcribing the savant side of my mind onto the chalkboard. It was 1968, about five years after great minds were making waves in mathematics with the *continuum hypothesis* about the possible sizes of infinite sets. I decided I would restate the hypothesis in relation to the cardinality of infinite sets, and started writing across the full length of the board, dragging Yeahwellah in lockstep with me like a magnet. He perused the work with a twitch here, a suck there, and a threatening wave of the wet rag at times too close to my important work for my liking, but he never interfered.

A screenshot of my passport to freedom follows:

The Cardinality of Infinite Sets and the Continuum Hypothesis.

\#   S1 represents **Rational Numbers**

\#   S2 represents **Integers**

\#   S3 represents **Real Numbers**

(All are examples of **infinite sets**.)

- Because S2 is a subset of S1, then the cardinality of S1 > the cardinality of S2
- Because S1 is a subset of S3, then the cardinality of S3 > the cardinality of S1
- Therefore the cardinality of S2 must be < the cardinality of S3

Applying *the continuum hypothesis*:

As S3 for Real Numbers has minimal possible cardinality, then the cardinality for S1 being Rational Numbers and expressed as 2 to the power of aleph-naught is > the cardinality of S2 for Integers expressed as aleph-naught and the cardinality of S3 for Real Numbers > the cardinality of S1.

THEREFORE there is no set S for which: aleph-naught < S < 2 to the power of aleph-naught.

- <u>So</u> there is a smaller cardinal number aleph-one which is > aleph-naught
- <u>And</u> 2 to the power aleph-naught = aleph-one.

As the throng of inmates gravitated towards my chalkboard masterpiece, I took a bow. Some clapped, others feigned wonder, one farted, and the rest gawked before drifting on. Yeahwellah stood his ground and marked out the territory as that of his disciple as if it was a sacred place and inviolable.

Invoking the sanctity of graffiti, nobody tampered with my exposé on the continuum hypothesis and it remained pristine within its borders for one whole week for all and sundry to gaze upon, ponder and marvel. It eventually came to the attention of someone that really mattered – the resident shrink. With my permission, he invited a group of three final year psychology students from Hoopla University to view my chalkboard summary. They took notes and one person photographed it. Afterwards they asked if I would meet with them for a chat in the cafeteria in the general hospital complex.

The two guys were quite gawky and all fingers and pencils, and quite insignificant. The girl, on the other hand, was enchanting and mesmerising but ephemeral, just as I imagined P.B. Shelley's *blithe Spirit* to be in his poem *To a Skylark*. We stood there staring open-mouthed at each other (the five of us including the psychiatrist), but it was 'Blithe Spirit', as I quickly dubbed her, who eventually articulated the ice-breaker.

'It's an honour and a privilege to talk with you, sir.' She curtsied and then offered me her hand. Now how's that for strange? I touched the tips of her fingers and kissed her hand ever so lightly before responding with a recital of the first four lines of the first stanza of Shelley's poem.

Hail to thee, blithe Spirit
Bird thou never wert,
That from Heaven, or near it
Pourest thy full heart

Her face took on a crimson hue that drained from her liquid lips left limpid as I continued:

Teach me half the gladness
That thy brain must know,
Such harmonious madness
From my lips would flow
The world should listen then, as I am listening now.

Everyone froze for a moment in response to my poetic utterances. Then, like a flock of pigeons released simultaneously or grace being dispensed at the dinner table, they all scraped chairs into positions around the coffee table and sat opposite me. It certainly killed the moment. I abandoned the use of verse and continued with a tone and text that I considered more appropriate to the situation.

'Well, here's your chance to talk to the lab rat. Prod me, poke me, put me under the microscope and see if you can work out why the big pharmaceutical companies need people like me. When you graduate, you will be doing their work for them, so you will need to have a rationale.'

There was no response so I continued, 'Working for No Man surrounded by pristine walls and under shuttered white light or in labs in No Man's Land, you will need to know who your clients are and what you can do for them.'

There was still no response. I continued with a few clues. 'Society prefers the world to be mediocre, passive, unthreatening, polite and preferably subservient.'

'Surely you don't believe that,' said Pencil Fingers like a lightning bolt being dispensed from a pencil sharpener.

'No, I just said it so Dr Freudfellow here can increase my dose of down-upper-down-downs. Gotta do my bit to keep the economy bubbling along nicely,' I replied.

Blithe Spirit reprimanded Pencil Fingers by reminding him that they were here to learn, not argue. I was entitled to express a point of view. As his hair bristled over Blithe Spirit's comment, I was quick to come to her rescue while allowing him to save face.

'Good point Blithe Spirit, but unfortunately lab rats don't have a point of view. Let me give you an example of how little we all know yet we pretend to know so much.' I turned and pointed to a painting on the opposite wall. 'Blithe Spirit … see that drawing of the dolphin on the wall?' I gestured. 'Could you please bring it over here.'

Blithe Spirit approached the counter and asked the proprietor if she could take down the painting so that we could study it. Meanwhile, I studied the way she walked, determined yet delicately. I listened to the way she talked, confident but quietly and gently. Bewitched, I watched her mouth and nose and ears and eyes and I wanted her to own me and make me smooth again.

The painting was not very large, but in her slender grasp, I imagined it was the Skylark carrying it. I leaped to my feet to take the load off her fragile frame, and as I sprang forth, Pencil Fingers almost fell off his chair. Maybe he assumed I was going to deck him or something, but although I would dearly have loved to do that, it was never my intention.

I placed the painting in the centre of the table and turned it slowly to face each of the other four. First, I turned to Blithe Spirit. 'Tell me what you see in this picture.'

'I see the blithe Spirit that Shelley speaks of in his poem *To a Skylark*.' Well, how could anyone fault that?

I looked at Pencil Fingers as I shifted the frame more towards him.

'The perspective is incredible. I don't know if you know much about art, but that's a quality painting.'

The third student was quite perplexed.

'I don't know much about art either, but I can see it's one print of only twenty in circulation so I assume that signature at the bottom of the painting must belong to a celebrated artist.'

My gaze turned to the resident shrink.

'Well, for what it's worth, I might as well put my twopence in. I see the dolphin frozen in flight as it breaks forth from the waves searching to escape from its own natural habitat. But like Sisyphus, it must return forever to its true station in life and hence I see a sadness there that might well reflect the way of the world as it is today. We all think the other man's grass is always greener, but it isn't and we must learn to accept our station in life and the cards with which we have been dealt.'

The students clapped and pretended they were impressed. Talk about wank.

'Well, I don't see any of those things,' I stated clearly. 'I'm a realist. Whether that artist is a celebrity, a clairvoyant, a master of perspective, or a poet doesn't concern me. What concerns me is the truth, and the truth is folks that the tail has been drawn the wrong way around.'

Second glances criss-crossed the painting and then eyeballed each other for confirmation as panic and fear of being caught short on knowledge began to set in. Not one of them had an answer to that.

'There's no artistic licence for that sort of thing. You see, it's all about ignorance. What your profession would call *ignorante*, pronounced *in-your-ont*; it's a French word. *Ignorante* is the opposite of *savant* which puts me in the *savant* category and you're all in the *in-your-ont* category … except for Blithe Spirit,' I added.

No clapping for the lab rat.

Then Blithe Spirit smiled at me; a smile that made me think there might be some worth in me after all. It reminded me that I needed a woman back in my life. Despite the pain of my past experience, I had to rise above it and not be ruled by it.

As we chatted, drank coffee and agreed never to agree, I began to absorb her benevolence, and for the first time in a long time I remembered what it was like to smile again. I was at peace and I was whole again. A little fresh kangaroo tail stew at last, and this time I was savouring it. They left and Blithe Spirit slipped me a note with a telephone number.

I was upgraded to 'fully-blown savant syndrome' by Dr Freudfellow and was out on a pension, given medication for whenever I felt depressed, and assigned a health worker who would visit me weekly until everyone was happy that I was self-medicating satisfactorily.

Bunch of cheapskates! I would have thought I was worth more than that.

CHAPTER 6

It's Blithe Spirit here and I need to say something in my own defence. After the session, I slipped the client a note with my telephone number written on it. I must admit this fellow has something about him that is hypnotic and mesmerising and I want to get to know him better. At arm's length, of course; patient–doctor code of ethics and all.

It's not a physical attraction in the sense of any suggestion of chemistry between us. No, our relationship, if you could call it that, would have to be strictly professional; at best platonic. From the moment I met him and gazed in awe at the clutter of mathematical assumptions and conclusions on that chalkboard, I could feel his pain. This stuttering individual was agony personified. Fully! It made me want to know him better; to understand his suffering and lighten his load; to hug him and make him better, and to help him conquer the demons inside his head.

After all, I said to myself, 'Isn't this what a psychologist is supposed to do? Whether I'm a student or a practitioner, identifying a need and addressing it must be a priority at all times. That's my rationale. If I'm afraid to confront the challenges facing traumatised minds, I might as well settle for reading romance novels or fantasising over how others resolve their dilemmas.'

When I read up on the client's case history, I only saw one side to him. In the flesh, however, he oozed hormones and masculinity; a dominant male. According to his own statement, after his detention in Cannabia, whether he was shit-faced on drugs and alcohol or not, he had an even greater problem with his expectations of loyalty, and the need for subservience from his beloved Penny Black who eventually broke his heart. He was obviously very intelligent but was his predisposition to deep thought a curse? Was Penny Black the problem or did he have a problem with women? Was his abuse as a child at the hands of his cruel stepfather so invasive as to cause him to distrust men, and did Penny Black's betrayal remove any gender bias and cause him to distrust everyone? Did his stutter juxtapose his manliness with a frailty that often accompanies fear?

How can I explain the gentle man I met who kissed my hand and quoted Shelley to me, who leaped up to defend me from the misogyny of my colleagues, and valued my point of view; who christened me Blithe Spirit and never even sought to know my name as if I didn't own one?

Yes, I did slip him a note. That was the least I could do to let him know I cared.

P.S. I thought I'd add this extra bit here just to keep all the facts together. After we got to know each other, and I'm talking months later, he often introduced me to others as 'his feminine side' – what he thought he would be like if he was born a woman. That meant we could never fall in love because that would entail him falling in love with himself. We used to joke about that whenever it came up. The irony was that he was in love with himself anyhow. He hated me calling him Narcissus. It showed I knew him better than he thought I did.

Aleph keeps a diary. He is meticulous. He records everything. He has no problem with me reading it. In fact, he feels it's the best way for me to keep up with what's going on inside his head. Sometimes I write a note in it if I decide it's the best way to message him about changes in his condition or circumstances. It allows him to digest it in his own time. Access to his diary certainly keeps me in the loop.

CHAPTER 7

As the first step in the beginning of my new life, I had my name changed to Aleph McNaught, a derivative of the *aleph naught* mathematical terminology referred to in the *continuum hypothesis*. I was able to rent a ramshackle old colonial with five rooms and wrap-around verandahs with the help of Blithe Spirit whose mother owned it but no longer lived there as she had dementia and had been institutionalised.

It was in Waking, a low socio-economic inner suburb of Hoopla where all hip young people gravitated to in the sixties. Blithe Spirit was worried that the house would be occupied by squatters if a permanent resident did not take responsibility for it. She offered it to me the first time I phoned her, and was so happy when I said 'yes' as it meant she no longer had to worry about it.

Surrounded by sex, drugs and rock-and-roll, I was quite *au fait* with all the character types I might expect to encounter. I was in my element basking in an unrestrained community where free speech, anti-war protesters, anarchists, religious cranks, doomsday sayers, vitamin munchers, dreadlocked hippies, free love and peace freaks abounded. It was a place where my sojourn in the wards of discontent, ill-intent and non-content would stand me in good stead. I had picked up so much about how to interact with people who rejected or avoided social norms or actually had some quite serious mental health issues.

I should mention at this point that the day I left the ward and changed my name to Aleph McNaught, my conscience began plaguing me. Yeahwellah lurked in the back of my mind. He didn't want me to leave because he had felt his calling for the first time in his life in my presence. In his eyes, I had become like the prophet Moses. I was one of God's chosen ones just like he saw himself as Jesus. That put me on the same pedestal as him. In fact, he believed that in the eyes of God I was probably a bit higher on the podium because Moses had delivered the Israelites from slavery in Egypt. Maybe the two of us had been chosen to deliver the broader population from the oppression and disadvantage that existed in Umbugumbuland. I would deliver them and he would forgive them their sins and die for them on the cross if necessary.

What reverberated in the back of my mind were the references to Moses and Jesus as if it was God calling out to me again. Most vividly I recalled the time I was stoned and my car had run out of petrol north of Cannabia. Anyhow, in the end, I had to promise that I would join him on his walk with God every Sunday. On the first Sunday visit, I found him so depressed he didn't even want to talk. By the second Sunday he had stopped eating, and by the third Sunday he was comatose. Rather than abandon him, I reconsidered my position as a citizen with a mission to reform the politics of the State. I realised I could and should do something for him.

As a representative of the Church, Yeahwellah could provide a buffer for that part of society that freaked out when God was brought into the equation. The last thing they wanted was for God to be left out of the equation. So Yeahwellah could take on an important complementary role in my new-world vision of what good government should be like. The Church and State would band together one day under my leadership and society would be all the better for it.

Yeahwellah came to live with me. He became a man of independent means (he too was put on a pension) and we became fused together. He was my shadow, always two paces behind or beside me as he adopted his new station in life. The Church and the State would remain as one until one or the other became superfluous. If I walked to the left, he walked to the left beside me. If I walked straight ahead, I lost him but I knew he was always two steps behind me. Only at night when I turned out the light did he leave me and sleep in his own bed in his own room. But he was back again the moment I woke up the next morning. It didn't bother me.

I charged him enough rent to cover the full rent of the house and he pitched in for half of all our living expenses. When I did the maths, I found it was true that two can live as cheaply as one. I was pleased with my decision to take Yeahwellah on board with me. I also looked after any spare money he had left over each pension day, and banked it in a trust account.

Blithe was ecstatic when I told her that I intended to use her mother's property as a halfway house for destitutes and desperadoes. She said her mother would be thrilled at the news. This didn't make a lot of sense to me because her mother was so out of it that she didn't know whether she was metal, stone, plant or animal.

Anyhow, by the time I had dredged the streets nearby to find suitable applicants and rented out the three other rooms, I was able to pay cash for a clapped-out VW Kombi van, known to the hippie community as a 'Splittie' because the front windscreen was divided down the centre by a metal bar. It belonged to a hippie who was hospitalised after several bouts of acute drug abuse and so burned out that he decided to leave Umbugumbuland and return to his native Suwajiland. There, 'where in summer the sun never sets' he hoped his rich parents would put him into rehab.

As a mechanic, I had the Kombi purring in no time at all, and the Suwaji was most impressed as I drove him to the airport. I even told him I was going to hot it up once I had more time and money, and that really made him happy. He said the car was like family to him and the only home he had known since he left Suwajiland. The strange thing was that before he went into the departure lounge, he hugged me and gave me all his Australian money, which was more than I had paid for the car. He stuffed the money in my shirt pocket for safe-keeping.

I was quite taken aback and hesitated while muttering 'Yeah … well … ah … well I was gonna say'.

Back in Camp McNaught in Waking where I lived, the financial side of things was looking up. When I did the math, I figured if I could double up on the beds in the other three rooms, I would be able to use the income to put a deposit on the colonial next door. While I was at it, if I put another six beds on the wrap-around verandah, I could put a deposit on a second colonial on the other side of Blithe Spirit's mother's property. I could then rent out those properties room by room to my ever-expanding clientele who were beginning to stream in from the countryside. At the same time, I applied to have those two properties subdivided, as they were on large blocks and each fronted onto two streets.

As some of the tenants became bored doing nothing, I bought paint and other materials and allowed them to 'artistically' refurbish the two properties. This made the properties even more attractive to people who were interested in living an alternative lifestyle, which in turn enabled me to put up the rent. When Blithe Spirit's mother died the following year, I offered to buy the property for a bargain price and had it subdivided and refurbished as well.

I was twenty-five years old before I reached this stage of becoming established, so to celebrate the event, I bought a print of Salvador Dali's *The Great Masturbator*. He was the same age as me when he painted that masterpiece, and it said as much about me as it did about him. I gave it pride of place above my work desk in my makeshift office in Waking. In so doing, I was reminding myself that I needed to keep a lid on my ambitions as it was all beginning to look like a bit of a wank.

Blithe Spirit and I became very close although we did not live together while she was still studying. She graduated with a psychology degree and went on to do her doctorate. For her thesis, she used me as a case study on the savant phenomena and was always in demand to speak at sociology and psychology conferences. She was offered a part-time lecturing position at Hoopla University which by this time had officially been granted international recognition.

In 1973, when I was twenty-six years old, I had bought another two colonials close to 'Camp McNaught' but on the opposite side of the street. I rented them out room by room as well. I then asked Blithe Spirit to live with me with the only condition being that Yeahwellah would have to come and live with us. I found a little red brick cottage in the upmarket suburb of Switcher which was a stone's throw from Hoopla University. It had a small granny flat attached where Yeahwellah could live. She agreed and praised me for my loyalty to Yeahwellah. She assured me that I had just made her the happiest girl in all Umbugumbuland. I would have done it earlier if I'd known she was going to accept. She was my ideal woman.

The house-warming was a simple occasion. All the guests were friends of Blithe's as I didn't have any friends except for Yeahwellah. When he asked to give a speech, you can imagine what he said and how long it took him to say it. We nearly had to gag him and bundle him into the broom cupboard because he was starting to drive everyone whambooty.

The strange thing is I have no photos of the house-warming event and there were no invitation cards or notices sent out to guests. I put it down to Blithe Spirit being such a private person.

CHAPTER 8

The best way to become fully involved in any pursuit is to be where the noise is. I rented an office in the main street of Hoopla Central. It was next door to the stock exchange building. There was a general mining boom in progress and everyone wanted to climb the money tree. Investors were doubling and even trebling their money in a matter of months.

I bought a print of Dali's *Geopoliticus Child Watching the Birth of a New Man* and placed it in the centre of the wall behind my new desk that had a clear view of the Hoopla River, which was in full flood. There was something symbolic about that event. It was a king tide and the river was backing up and threatening to break its banks. I was afraid I might become the river.

Equidistant around that painting were hung my other favourite Dali prints. They were *Head Exploding, Galatea of the Spheres, Soft Self-Portrait with Fried*

Bacon, The Persistence of Memory, The Temptation of Saint Anthony, Dream Caused by the Flight of a Bee, The Disintegration of the Persistence of Memory, Lobster Telephone, The Anthropomorphic Cabinet, Spain, Sleep, Spider of the Evening, Swans Reflecting Elephants, Melting Watch, Elephants, Bacchanale, Metamorphosis of Narcissus and *Landscape with Butterflies.* The rest of the wall was bare. It was Dali's Wall. It was me. Dali the realist who could only express himself by being surreal, and I the lost sheep who could only express himself through absurd thought and saying what everyone else perceived as claptrap.

The prints represented the eighteen waking hours of my day when I exercised my fractured mind to fund my quest to shore up the foundations of a political pathway fatigued by centuries of misuse and needing a new way forward that would lead towards the greater good.

Apart from the blue-chip stocks like the banks, insurance companies, media and telecommunication companies, and the huge mining companies like AGO, Mount Mega Mines, Liquid Gold Corporation and Gold Pit Inc., there was a host of penny-dreadful stocks, speculative oil and mining companies being listed on the stock exchange daily. These companies used proceeds from initial public offerings (IPOs) based on a prospectus that the brokers peddled to their money-hungry clients. One stockbroker had made so much money, he bought a Rolls Royce and had it gold-plated. That became the benchmark I set for myself.

Land had also doubled in price. I sold the five blocks I had subdivided off in Waking to fund my stock market investments. I went to lectures and seminars and read books and attended tutorials for months on end. I met brokers every day and lunched with them until I felt confident that I was ready to begin investing. Oil and gas, gold and nickel IPOs were all the rage in the early seventies, so I selected several companies and began investing quite heavily in them. In the first three months, all of them except one, Neptune Nickel, went down quite a lot, and that's when I first realised that some branches of the money tree actually had thorns.

As the value of my portfolio of shares shrank and began to vaporise before my eyes, I found myself peering into the jaws of the *Jabberwock* waiting to be cracked open and my innards sucked out and worked over like a cow chewing its cud. Well, if that's not enough to make a sane person go mad, imagine what it was doing to panic-prone me. I became this toy soldier trying to scramble out of a cooking pot ten times my size and shaped like a steel wok with greasy sides. It was run, struggle, drop to all fours and grasp up the side of the wok without a grappling hook for the lip, only to slip, slide and career back to the bottom like a boy with his bum on cardboard sliding down a sand dune.

I asked my broker Ted Treredneck what was going on; why my stocks were going down. Ted was one of those where if words were money he dreaded the thought of even spending a cent.

'More sellers than buyers,' he suggested. WooHoo! Déjà vu of kangaroo tail stew and little black sheep drowning. It was time to play *mea culpa* to explain it all to myself so I could live with the imminent disaster that was about to befall me and claim my substantial fortune.

I convinced myself that I only invested in shares because I needed to make big money fast to self-fund and stake my claim to a political future. I worried that the real reason was that I had become greedy and a dirty little capitalist. Was politics just a cover-up tale or rationale for a get-rich-quick game that was going horribly wrong? I'd played get-rich-quick games before and they worked well. Why wasn't it working well now? I asked Yeahwellah whether he thought it was a case of 'God giveth and God taketh away' but he just started uttering monosyllables that never amounted to an answer. Great contribution the Church was making to the Church and State tag team!

Was I afraid of returning to where I started, living day by day as a *povvo*? Was that so bad, anyhow? Was it Blithe who was really motivating me to make a go of my life? Was the quest for wealth and power a right for the chosen few or a universal human right? I was a fraud and flawed and I wanted to prove I could make a difference despite being 'different'. Or was it my difference that had brought me bad luck and misfortune just like it did to most people who were different? The fact that I never knew my father proved how rotten my luck really was.

One Monday morning I awoke to the news that Neptune Nickel Limited had been placed in a trading halt pending an announcement. I paid no attention to it. That afternoon I ambled across to the exchange next door to find people rushing to and fro and the whole floor buzzing with movement, with murmur and callers all wanting their share of the action.

In those days, the exchange used the post system whereby stocks and transactions were recorded in chalk on boards or 'posts' next to a three or four-letter code identifying each company. Two 'chalkies' continually rushed along beside the blackboards recording or altering bids, offers and sales.

I glanced at the code NNL for Neptune Nickel Limited and noticed the share had jumped from 70 cents to $7.30 before it was placed in the trading halt. I couldn't believe it. It was what they called a ten-bagger in local share parlance, meaning the share had risen to ten times its long-term trading price. I phoned Ted, and after waiting for over five minutes without getting through, I decided to walk up the three fights of stairs to his office to ask about the reason for the price surge.

'More buyers than sellers,' he called out from his office in his usual laconic monotone. Great help he was, but I could see that he was busy so I returned to the floor of the exchange in the hope of gleaning some news on the stock there. It was just before closing time, yet in the short time that I was away, the stock had leaped another $1.30 to $8.60. It closed at $9.40. I had already done the maths on the trot several times, and each time the result was that I was making big money. My mind was in a computing frenzy.

The front page and the business section of the next day's papers made the reason quite clear – the company had intersected a major nickel laterite ore deposit suitable for open cut mining at its mine at Wangaloo in Western Province. I had made a significant investment of 10,000 shares in the company at 50 cents and it was suddenly worth $94,000. My whole portfolio, including the losers, cost me $20,000, so I was already loads ahead on my initial outlay.

Throughout the rest of the week, that discovery unleashed a feeding frenzy on the market, especially in nickel stocks. By Friday of the first week, the stock was listed with buyers at $27.60 and no sellers. That meant my holding in Neptune Nickel alone was worth $276,000. All the muscles in my body were going into fibrillation. I refused to sell, joking with Ted that I would only sell when each share fetched ten times that much.

'Put me down as a seller at $276, Ted,' I called out to him after he had finished.

'You gotta be dreaming,' was his reply.

That discovery created the largest mineral boom that Umbugumbuland had ever experienced. Week after week, Ted kept encouraging me to sell. At $45, he said it couldn't go any higher as there were no more results, only speculation and rumour. I said 'no'. At $63 he said it was ridiculous and someone claimed that the prospector who made the find and staked out the tenements had a bit of a dodgy past. He suggested I sell. I said 'no'. At $96 a share he said that he would stake his life on the share not reaching $100 because just before that, the stock would retrace and possibly come back to $50. He suggested I sell. I said 'no'. He suggested I sell half. I said 'no'. The share came back to $82 and he said he had told me so and that I should sell before it went back to $50. I said 'no'. The following week it opened at $120 and quickly went to $175 a share. He was breathless. All he could manage was a whisper.

'Sell ... sell ... please sell some.' He was begging me now.

'Ted, my price is $276 ... no more and no less. Please don't ask me again and that's my final word on the matter. If you value our friendship and your business, don't ask me again until you get that price and then sell the lot.' I hung up.

Those were the words of a smartarse upstart. I'm ashamed of them and I deserved to lose everything the moment I said that. It was hubris at its worst, uncalled for and unjustifiable. It was inviting ill will after the goodwill God had bestowed upon me. You know, Jack was right; I was an ingrate. Tweetie was right; I was too smart for my own good. I was right; 'I'm a conniving son-of-a-bitch'.

For four months, the stock kept climbing,

retracing and then climbing again. Early in the fifth month after the discovery, Ted called me.

'Aleph, Aleph … is that you Aleph?'

'Yes, Aleph here, Ted. I thought I told you not to call me,' I reminded him.

'Aleph … I've sold your entire holding in Neptune Nickel Limited at $276 per share for a total of $2.76 million. Congratulations Aleph! You are now officially a millionaire in cold, hard cash … minus my commission, of course.' He then let out an almighty yell and hung up. I went across to the bar next door to the stock exchange and bought two bottles of the best quality champagne, ambled across to his building and up the stairs to his office where the entire staff stood back and clapped as I popped the corks out of the bottles of champers, pinched the plastic cups from the water cooler and shared the wine with all my newfound friends.

The share reached $280 per share a few days later and then began plummeting for no reason other than 'herd mentality', as the analysts labelled the phenomena. It finally stabilised again and eventually, the price of nickel collapsed and the company was delisted from the stock exchange within three years. Neptune Nickel Limited produced 8 million tonnes of nickel. You've got to be lucky, sometimes, but I insist my decisions were all based on sound judgement; hubris aka wank.

The truth is I understood herd mentality. I ran with the herd on the way up, but kept to the outside so that I wouldn't be trampled when it turned on itself and began running in the opposite direction. Not a bad investment (and good timing I might add) by 'a crazy from the back blocks'. Even Ted agreed with me.

'So, you're trying to tell me you think I'm crazy are you, Ted?'

'You've never been anything but. Only a crazy person could hold out for that long because a rational person would have got out at $27. A decision to hold out at every price upward from that exemplified and was directly proportional to the level of insanity of the decision maker.'

'Savant syndrome, my friend. Look it up sometime,' I responded superciliously.

CHAPTER 9

That collapse did not deter investors from seeking out the next big Neptune Nickel. They re-entered the market with a vengeance, pouncing on every IPO on mining and oil stocks irrespective of any of the fundamentals. Everyone, including long-term supposedly astute investors, was caught up in the exuberance of the moment. They began to sell their properties to fund their forays into the stock market just as I had done with my Waking subdivisions. They all had dreams of lighting up cigars with $100 bills. The running of the bulls with their thundering hoofs could be heard resonating down Main Street towards the stock exchange building where I was already on the footpath looking for an alcove to avoid being gouged.

I found several 'alcoves' in the old heritage buildings offered up for a pittance in the central business district of Hoopla. Admittedly, they needed maintenance and a cosmetic facelift, but nothing a few repairs, replacement windows and a lick of paint couldn't fix. I bought three buildings one street back from the main street in Hoopla Central. I knew that if I spruced them up and presented them well, they would fetch better returns and longer term loyal customers. The bricks were sandblasted to remove the dust and grime of decades of exposure to the elements. All the window spaces were refitted with the latest materials, and trims were scraped back to bare timber and repainted with bright colours. Within weeks of the buildings being available for rent, huge mining companies brimming with excess funds from the mining boom signed long leases and paid premium rentals to use them for their head offices.

I allotted another huge portion of my stock market gains to the purchase of new subdivisions zoned industrial and commercial on the immediate outskirts north, east, south and west of the city centre. I figured that as the city expanded, small businesses would keenly seek those positions. Long term there was also potential for them to be rezoned high-rise. Those properties would become my retirement nest-egg.

I engaged building companies to erect suitable structures that boasted aesthetically designed frontages with areas allocated for small gardens planted with flowers and decorative shrubs. Small businesses snapped up these too for rental as the snowballing effect of the outflow of cash from the mining boom boosted the economy which in turn fuelled the demand for goods and services.

Through these good times my Yeahwellah was beginning to lose his missionary zeal but he kept his position glued to my hip and became very protective of me. He rarely spoke anymore because he realised that it was impacting my patience. Instead, he applied himself to his new role as driver of the company car and as my virtual bodyguard. Blithe Spirit was content at her work and rarely became involved with my business ventures or my personal life for that matter. It was as if she had found a little nook at the back of my brain and was hibernating in there away from any interaction that might impact either way on our relationship.

I myself continued to wrestle with that dark period in my past when I was brutally abused both mentally and physically and scarred by the ghoulish love affair. I shudder at the thought of being incarcerated and humiliated by people far less intelligent than me and who were disrespectful of me. Sometimes the recall of those bad events would cause my brain to frazzle to the point that I became withdrawn, depressed and fearful for my sanity. Yeahwellah knew when I was ensnared in one of those moods, and it was a great comfort to me knowing that he was there on standby, watching over me like Jesus, allowing me time to collect my thoughts and reboot my brain. Blithe Spirit, on the other hand, did not sense this frailty that caused me to cocoon my activities and interaction with others. She seemed to assume that it was just the pressure of work and paid no attention to the symptoms. It was as if she didn't care and it reminded me of the way my mother stood aside and did nothing as Jack beat me. Maybe some perception of an ironclad exterior made them believe I was immune from it all but there was a lot of mush and a lot of hurt beneath that armour.

As I came through each period of depression, I became stronger just knowing that I had survived it, and my resolve became more focused. However, I began to miss the excitement and the adrenaline hits that playing the stock market afforded me. It was ultimately a form of gambling – just another addiction – another way of getting beaten up, without the bruises. The ecstasy of winning and the agony of losing had no differentiation when it came to adrenaline flow. The constant nevertheless was always there; judgement was impaired. In hindsight, my stubborn insistence on waiting for my Neptune Nickel shares to go to $276 was driven not by good judgement but by madness. Maybe I was afraid of the thought of winning when karma decreed that I should always be a loser. Maybe my reticence to sell was that I was waiting to lose it all. I was supposed to be the cursed one with the rotten luck who never knew his father, and I didn't want to have to give up that underprivileged situation tag. How ridiculous was that? Ted was right, that was crazy and there was no way I would ever do it again.

Well, that's what I believe today. Who knows what I might do tomorrow? You see, there are times when I'm trapped in a virtual reality capsule. Inside, looking out is like looking through a translucent luminous eggshell where the focus of the eye dissolves so that there is no longer a world outside. I am ensnared in my own little world where the embryo I'm floating in nurtures me. I crack the shell and in the mirror I become Dali's *Geopoliticus Child Watching the Birth of a New Man* launched into his world of oblong melting landscapes, obelisks, elephants and horses with sinewy elongated legs, leaping tigers, propped-up heads with phased-out bodies, a tired dog on crutches, heads exploding beside his swans reflecting elephants in a pond. The butterflies carry my battered body out of his deformed world. Their double helix wings represent the presence of God in my life as I parachute back to earth.

In that world, I'm not even sure whether I own those 10,000 shares of Neptune Nickel, and strangely I don't care. At moments like those, I own nothing and am beholden to nobody. I just want to lie there numb, in limbo, just like I did when Jack bashed me unconscious at home or Tom the Toad's deputy dog left me in my cell to wallow in my vomit on a mattress on the cold concrete floor. It's where I cease to feel the pain and that sensation of inner peace is greater than any other feeling I have ever known. In fact, I suspect only death can eclipse that feeling, and that is why I have never feared death. For in death, I see *nirvana*.

To indulge in my passion for risk-taking, my broker Ted invited me to a seminar on equity options trading. The Umbugumbuan Options Market had recently been established on the stock exchange. It involved derivatives trading on a selected number of blue chip (top listed, expensive and supposedly quality) stocks. Equity options are the most common type of derivatives trading. They provide the right, but not the obligation, to buy (call) or sell (put) a quantity of stock. One contract equals 100 shares of stock at a set price (strike price), within a set period (prior to the expiration date). For this privilege, you pay a premium on each share bought, and that is all you have to outlay on the stock. The advantage of derivatives trading is that it allows you to control tens of thousands of dollars of stock for a relatively small outlay and you can make big money irrespective of whether the market goes up or down. The potential for profit is huge but the potential for loss of that premium is also huge if the stock goes in the opposite direction to the one you anticipated.

I was hooked from the first seminar. It was the closest thing to six-shooter roulette that I could imagine without the brains on the floor alongside any bloodbath. All you lost was your money and/or your sanity. Well, I figured I had already lost my sanity. I tell you, sometimes I'm teetering on the edge of an abyss where echoes from across the chasm beckon me to leap and sleep with them on sound waves woven into hammocks in the sky.

Anyhow, I didn't go into derivative trading all willy-nilly. Again, I took my time. I read stories about the pitfalls. I knew the risks. What I had was a relatively cheap way of pitting my intellect against the world's best in the equity investment realm. They had the shares and I had the leverage whereby, if I played it right, I could turn the tables on them so that I got the shares and they ended up with jack shit. That would finally get me that gold-plated Rolls Royce I was after. I couldn't wait to enter the fray.

One day I left the office early to check if Blithe Spirit was still living with me. When I found she was not at home, I panicked. I turned around to check if Yeahwellah knew where she might be but he wasn't there either. That made me very suspicious and I suddenly had visions of Blithe Spirit running off with Yeahwellah. I couldn't remember how I had gone home from the office because the car wasn't there. I went back into the house and the walls began closing in on me. I worked out that if I backed myself into a corner and sat under the glass topped table, the walls would eventually jam up against the table and at least I wouldn't get squashed. When the ceiling began descending, I feared the hell that was in store for me with my claustrophobia. I started praying. I recited passages from the Bible, and in one last-ditch effort, raised my arms like Moses and commanded the walls and the ceiling to recede.

Jesus appeared before me and everything began to rewind. I came out from under the table and ran towards the bright light that was the apparition of Jesus in the doorway, and I knew I had been saved.

Well, it was Jesus, but not the real Jesus. It was

Yeahwellah. I threw myself at him and hugged him. I could hear him muttering and felt him struggling a bit but I didn't want to let him go in case I lost him again. He was patient and I soon regained my composure. He gave me some water and then some tablets. When he left to use the telephone, I grabbed the bottle and read the label. It was the medication that he took every day for himself. I felt calm then a cloud with a silver halo attached itself to me. A time-lapse sensation followed of me going in and out of consciousness. Blithe Spirit appeared on the wings of a skylark. I thought I must be dead. She was beside herself with worry and kept asking Yeahwellah so many questions that his tongue became entangled in a thousand knots saying nothing that made any sense to her. Then he handed her the bottle of tablets.

'What? Have you overdosed on these?' she screamed at me.

'No Blithe Spirit, I just took two tablets and I'm a lot better already,' I lied.

Blithe embraced me and hugged me tightly.

'Good man … smart man,' she almost whispered as a way of apologising for having screamed at me a moment earlier.

Anyhow, after that episode, Blithe Spirit prescribed more medication. It made me feel better but it clouded my judgement. Within a week, I lost $35,000 on my derivative investments and I couldn't be sure whether it was $35,000 or $350,000. I didn't want to ask

Ted because he would have thought I was losing my mind. I told Blithe Spirit about my predicament (losing my judgement, not the amount of money) but she insisted I keep taking the medication or the little men in white overalls would come and put me in a double plastic wrap and take me away.

I realised after a month of bad decisions I would have to go off my medication. Within a week, I could feel my confidence coming back and there were no signs of the fog that had enveloped my brain during that last episode. I took a liking to a silver, lead and zinc mining company called Mount Mega Mining with the code MMM. Unsure whether I had lost $35,000 or $350,000 on my previous derivatives trading venture, I decided to buy *calls* in MMM with the intention of making $350,000 and recouping what I might have lost previously. I did exactly what I said I wouldn't do ever again after my ridiculous decision to hold Neptune Nickel until the stock reached $276.

This time around it was all luck. Within two weeks, a takeover offer was made for MMM at a 33% premium, and as I was highly leveraged, my calls skyrocketed. The moment I picked up the phone call from Ted, I said 'sell' without waiting for him to tell me anything.

'But this is one time when you shouldn't sell,' he pleaded with me. 'There might be a counter offer and you stand to make megabucks.'

I repeated, 'Sell,' and hung up the phone. Ted

knew what that meant.

Next day, he phoned me again.

'Good thing you sold; there has been no counter offer and now there is a concern that the sale may not go through as it is pending a review from the Foreign Investment Review Board. The stock has dropped right back. You are about $350,000 up on your whole derivatives portfolio since you started trading.'

How's that for maths? I was happy with that.

'Buy the calls back again for the whole amount of the profit but extend the expiration date out one month,' I said and hung up. He didn't even call me back to object.

Two days later, a counter offer came through from an Umbugumbuan mining giant and the share price of MMM skyrocketed just as Ted said it might before I ignored him last time. I was a wreck but I made $13.5 million on that deal. I was rich enough to realise my dream of a gold-plated Rolls Royce.

When I thought about it, I realised I was different. As a contrarian, why would I buy a Rolls Royce and gold-plate it when somebody else had already done it? No, I decided instead to buy the run-down Gumbu Guru Hotel which was a One Star virtual boarding house with a liquor licence. Its three greatest drawcards were position, position and position, right at the top end of Main Street near the river and opposite the botanic gardens. I demolished it and built a hotel/casino complex, and financed it with my windfall from the calls on MMM. I applied for and was granted a casino licence and renamed it the Gumbu Guru Hotel Casino Complex.

I had put Hoopla on the world map, and soon tourists began trickling into the city and spending their money on cultural artefacts, in restaurants and on accommodation. Any money they had left over was usually lost in the casino, but they left the city happy and told all their friends about it. Within two years, I had bought another hotel and refurbished it. The popularity of the casino guaranteed an almost 100 per cent occupancy rate. I renamed it *The Blithe Spirit* and the emblem beneath the name was a skylark with wings fully extended.

My time was now fully occupied looking after the casino and refurbishing *The Blithe Spirit*. I decided to go back to purchasing equities rather than playing the market with derivatives. With equities, there was no expiration date for the investment, so all I had to do was park my money there and collect the dividends, which was easier than collecting rent.

Unbelievably, the stock market rose almost uninterrupted for ten years from 1976. My share portfolio just kept growing as I took up the offers to reinvest all the dividends at discounts to the market price and without paying any brokerage.

On another front, a low-lying area close to the ocean on the eastern seaboard was mooted by the Hoopla City Council as an ideal location for an international airport. I saw this as a wonderful opportunity to diversify my investments as a land developer. After all, it was just an extended form of real estate investment where I had enjoyed great success in the past, except on a larger scale. It would provide me with an interest and the intellectual challenge side-stepping the high stress, high-roller avenues for making money like casinos and stock markets.

I needed to set my thinking to a developer's mindset. I have played this game before and it had served me well. For example, when my state of mind became a matter of concern to me, I set my thinking to a psychologist's mindset. I taught myself to think like they did. There was nothing about Blithe that I hadn't already discovered for myself. The savant syndrome was my idea. The *trample therapy theory*, which I'll tell you about later and proved to be ground-breaking psychological concept, was simply the antivenin for surviving violence and abuse. I had worked that out long before Blithe tagged it with some intellectual jargon. Yeahwellah became my religious mindset mojo. As my shadow, I could position myself at any time to have him there when I needed him or to make him vanish as easily as turning off the light that casts the shadow.

For my land developer mindset, I built it around a character who often lost his money gambling at my casino. I nicknamed him 'Scupper' after the sailor dog in the children's story *Scupper the Sailor Dog*, because of the resilience he displayed in the face of great adversity. A high roller, he could lose $10,000 at the casino without batting an eyelid, twitching an earlobe, vibrating a sensitive neck vein or flinching a muscle. Imagine what he could do when trying to clinch a business deal. He was a master at bluff while flush with business acumen. He had the expertise and I had the money so I suggested we combine as an alliance that would thrust us into the big league. If he agreed to exchange venues from gambling in the casino to this new venue where the thrill of the chase was equally exciting, the venture promised more highs than a junkie on morphine life support.

I agreed to put up all the cash, but when it came to fulfilling my part of the bargain, my bank would not come to the party.

'This development game is a very risky business. With airports, if something goes wrong, you can't resell it, because it's a swamp and nobody would want to buy it,' my banker of twelve good years standing warned me.

'But you have plenty of collateral with all my other businesses,' I argued.

'It's not about collateral, it's about funding and at the moment we have billions of dollars in share market margin loans. The only way we would entertain lending you money for such a project would be for you to divest your entire share portfolio and put that money into the development.'

'But my share market portfolio is in take-off at the moment. I don't want to liquidate it,' I protested, but my words were falling on deaf ears.

My banker refused to budge and I phoned Ted

and told him to sell my entire portfolio of shares. He didn't argue, he just did it. And while he was at it, he convinced the banker to sell his entire portfolio of shares as well. Think about it. Who was giving who advice here?

It was August 1987 and I was on the cusp of my fortieth birthday on October 19. The day I sold my whole portfolio, the stock market spiked upwards like you wouldn't believe. Then it retraced a little before spiking even higher. It did this a few more times, and each time the market kept going higher. I was beginning to curse my banker for imposing his will on my business decisions. My banker wasn't too happy either, but when he asked Ted why the market was going up so sharply, Ted gave him his stock answer.

'More buyers than sellers.' What else would you expect?

On October 19 when life was supposed to begin for people who turned forty, (according to conventional wisdom) it suddenly stopped for thousands of over-committed stock market investors. In one trading day, stock market prices around the world crashed between 22% and 25%, causing complete chaos, shock and awe. After thanking God that I had liquidated my portfolio just in time, I phoned my banker who felt the same way about having liquidated his portfolio.

'I knew I was doing the right thing when I decided to follow your decision,' he added.

'Yeah, well that wasn't my decision. You told me I had to liquidate or else you wouldn't approve the loan for the airport development.'

'Maybe, but you still made the decision,' he insisted.

'Well, if you put it that way, then I guess so. What on earth do you reckon caused the market to crash like that?' I asked.

'Well, according to *The Book of Ted*, it was more sellers than buyers,' he responded calmly.

'Are you going to buy back in?' he added eagerly.

'Nah … I figure we should see how this one pans out,' I suggested.

In the next three months, the market fell a further 20%. And just after New Year, I was confronted by the face of an old mentor of mine making front page news in *The Hoopla Daily*. It was the man with the gold-plated Rolls Royce. He had jumped from the ninth floor of the Hoopla Stock Exchange Building.

CHAPTER 10

The tragic death of my mentor unnerved me a bit. I kept having nightmares and every time the body at the base of the building was turned over for identification, it was my face that I saw. One day, I was in my office with my back to Dali's paintings, and through my window, a comet-like object with a blue fiery tail hurtled towards me from beyond the blue. Personified, it had the face of Dali's *Galatea of the Spheres*. At supersonic speed, it was in the zone of silence. As it passed directly overhead, the sound barrier was breached, and there was a glass-shattering, walls-creaking, roof-lifting, floor-buckling, head-exploding sonic boom. Greater than any sound I had known, it took my consciousness away.

I was left floating in its wake like a cotton tree seed on its bioparachute, tossed around on the whim of the wind, with its currents and eddies defying gravity over and over again.

These phenomenological experiences started doubling up on me and I often became disorientated. Sometimes I wasn't sure whether I was asleep or awake. One day I was so confused, I got Yeahwellah to take me home knowing Blithe Spirit would be at work. I became lost. I needed a way out of this haunting; some sort of exorcism. I chose Yeahwellah as my exorcist. He would plead with God for my forgiveness. I had never done anything like this before because I never believed I was ever guilty of anything. Maybe I was wrong. Otherwise why would this be happening to me?

I had long since given up going to church although I studied the Bible every night and recited passages whenever a dilemma or a crisis of confidence confronted me. I suddenly had an epiphany. I knew exactly what I had to do. Yeahwellah looked on in bewilderment as I leaned the extension ladder against the side of the house and climbed up on to the roof. Yeahwellah was a complete wreck and didn't know what to do with his hands. He was unable to think of something to say, unwilling to risk upsetting me. He placed his mouth over his right hand between the thumb and the index finger, bit into it and started shaking it like a rag doll. The terror in his eyes was a laser that locked onto mine. I raised my eyes skywards, and extending both arms, began my communion with God from the rooftop.

I recited passages from the Bible. I shouted out the story of Moses who after forty days and forty nights returned from Mt Sinai with the Ten Commandments from God, only to find that his people had betrayed him and turned their faith to the worship of the golden calf. I begged God for forgiveness and asked Him to punish me accordingly or bring His wrath down upon me and destroy me like He did the worshippers of the god of the golden calf.

Then I heard God talking back to me.

He called out 'Moooooooooses ... Mooooooses ...' just as I'd heard when I was lost in the sheep country that time out the back of Cannabia. I then realised it wasn't God but Yeahwellah dressed in a white toga scrambling up the ladder and across the corrugated iron roof towards me. By the time he reached me, he was talking in tongues. This was a sure sign to me that he was conveying a message from God. I had to listen but I couldn't make any sense of it. My knees buckled, and though I was still conscious, I collapsed. He crawled towards me on his knees, lifted me on to his lap and cradled me.

Well, that's the way it was with me. I certainly wasn't doing it to impress anybody although I certainly got plenty of attention that day. Half the neighbourhood, fire brigade, police and ambulance were all circling the house waiting for me, and especially Yeahwellah, to do something stupid.

Luckily, Blithe Spirit had just returned from work. The police pressed no charges against me but they took Yeahwellah away for creating a public nuisance. Blithe

Spirit admonished me after she found out I had not been taking my medication for two months. That's all I admitted to her. It was more of a white lie than a deliberate lie because I didn't want to hurt her or disappoint her.

I went back on the regular medication, especially for the whole time Yeahwellah was readmitted to the ward at Hoopla General Hospital. These days it was referred to as 'the respite centre'.

I began to feel much better, and although a bit dopey, I had enough money. I didn't really need to work anymore. I decided to stop work and play golf. This was on Blithe Spirit's advice and she was delighted when I agreed to do it.

Meanwhile, I visited Yeahwellah every day in the respite centre. On the third day he took a heavy glass ashtray and threw it through the television screen because the newsreader was interrupting his prayer session. I knew he would have no trouble after that. In fact, there was no retribution from the staff. He became quite happy in there. It was like a cleansing for him. He felt revitalised in doing God's work, except this time many of the inmates gathered willingly around him and listened like preschool children as he spoke. The heavy glass ashtray did not shatter like the television screen, so he reclaimed it and filled it with 'holy water' which he used to baptise and bless his 'disciples'. Thereafter, the glass ashtray became a symbol of their faith; a gleaming indestructible emerald jewel.

Within a week of agreeing to give up work, I decided that rather than give up work, I would try my hand at something different. I approached Scupper about the possibility of building a world-class golf course along the oceanfront near the international airport that we were building. All the equipment needed for pumping sand was right there on hand. The economy of scale made the project a natural progression of our business partnership. It simply involved building a huge canal to drain the swamp between the airport and the oceanfront, and channelling the water into the river that bisected the city of Hoopla and emptied into the sea.

Over 200 hectares of swamp to the north of the proposed golf course fed into the low-lying areas to the south at the site of the airport under construction. It was a breeding ground for mosquitoes and the community council was forever being harangued to do something about it. I had a solution that would solve the council's problem. It would also help alleviate the looming land for housing crisis brought on by the huge influx of population bearing down on the new gambling mecca that was Hoopla City. Hoopla was being promoted as a 'down-and-out' tourist destination (my idea) that was forever bathed in sunshine, had a cool climate, and had beautiful beaches surrounding it to the north and south. Talk about suckers; if it was advertised as 'up-and-coming', nobody would have been interested, but the 'down-and-out' tag brought in the rat-pack generation who were flush with money but bored shitless and needed some carefree sounding incentives to get them to check out the place.

Anyhow, back to the business proposition. If this water source could be contained and its natural flow drained off, the cost of the drainage of the airport region, as well as the golf course development area, would be reduced markedly. I proposed turning that swamp into a mega canal estate development for the rich and famous. After all, they usually only had two pastimes – playing golf and travelling. Access to the ocean from the estate would be a major drawcard catering to their third great love of sail boats, ocean-going yachts and vessels to enhance their celebrity status.

All I had to do was convince Scupper that it was his idea and get him to do all the work and oversee the complete project. I arranged for the money supply while Scupper lapped up the challenge to occupy his mind and indulge his creativity. Day and night, he never left his office in the swamp. His gambling days were over. He was a prisoner of his own passion just like Yeahwellah, and I was his custodian.

***

To appease Blithe Spirit after reneging on giving up work, I suggested financing a clinic where she and a dedicated team of professionals could work on putting into practice an innovative therapy (the product of my psychologist mindset alluded to earlier) involving trampling. The therapy offers a substitution for deliberate self-harm or parasuicidal tendencies (like me slashing my wrists or trying to poke out my right eye during the Penny Black affair) exhibited by people with personality disorders. Instead of the person engaging in self-harm as a coping mechanism to continue to live rather than end their life, a dedicated professional utilises *trample therapy* to appease the patient. The therapy can also function to alleviate intense emotional pain or distress, overwhelming negative feelings, thoughts or memories (like those I experienced during my childhood).

To understand it, you need to know the risk factors for people engaging in self-injury. It might not be a nice topic for the faint-hearted, but you need to know. The main risk factor is a mental disorder like depression or anxiety. Other risk factors include the misuse of drugs and alcohol, low self-esteem covered up by bravado, poor social problem-solving skills, and an internalised sense of hopelessness. From what you have read so far, you already know I have them all, so I have a lot of self-interest invested in the relief this therapy has to offer.

All Blithe Spirit had to do was apply the jargon needed to communicate the theory behind it all so that the practitioner would not be branded a charlatan, a quack, a sham, a fraud, a fake, a pretender or plain downright kinky.

Blithe practised the *trample therapy* on me. You can think of it as a form of massage. I lay on a thin mattress on the floor while the practitioner firstly appeased the 'demon spirits' afflicting the patient by applying the gentlest of fingertip taunting of the skin, especially on the scalp and body extremities. This can be up to three hours of stroking until the only sensation is a breath of air delivered in silence. At various intervals, the 'demon spirits' dissolve and are drawn away by an invisible draught that caresses the body, creating a cooling effect that is the signal for the practitioner to begin to apply bodyweight to the patient. This is done with the foot or feet to maximise weight with minimum movement. As the pressure on the body mounts, the rush of blood to the point of contact invites complete surrender. The weight melts into the bones of your arms, hands and legs. It fills your stomach and compresses your chest as your lungs pump the cavity full and you cry out 'I have your measure. Jump if you dare!'. Then there is the head – an exercise in living dangerously for both the patient and the practitioner. The brain regresses into the compressed skull and the horrors are squeezed out of hiding like air from a bicycle pump. Clean, fresh thoughts are sucked back in as the pressure comes off and the psyche is cleansed.

John Keats describes the feeling well in *Ode to a Nightingale:*

> *My heart aches, and a drowsy numbness pains*
> *My sense, as though of hemlock I had drunk*
>
> ...
>
> *Darkling I listen; and, for many a time*
> *I have been half in love with easeful Death*
> *Call'd him soft names in many a mused rhyme,*
> *To take into the air my quiet breath;*
> *Now more than ever seems it rich to die*
> *To cease upon the midnight with no pain.*

Now you have it.
No, you don't!

CHAPTER 11

It's me again, Blithe. Understanding Aleph can tend to become a bit complex so I thought I should step in and try to explain some things about him that you need to know to understand him better. I wanted to get to understand him better because there are so many people out there that are misunderstood. For you it might be just a curiosity, but for me trying to understand people is part of my job.

I have had many discussions with Aleph in relation to state-of-mind issues. He is always adamant he knows more about it than all the professors at the universities at home and abroad. Now that's a pretty sweeping statement, but that's Aleph. He's such a know-all.

He has always been particularly concerned about suicide, parasuicide and the notion of self-harm as exit pathways for people who are traumatised or have experienced trauma in the past and know of no other way to cope with it. His simple logic could be hard to fault at times:

Your bowels are full ... you shit.
Your bladder is full ... you piss.
Your head is fucked ... you self-harm.

It helped me understand masochism.

Aleph had a state-of-mind theory on sanity and insanity. He said he would dumb it down for me so that I would find it easier to comprehend. He can be so condescending, that guy. Anyhow, it made sense, so I thought it was worth passing on. It certainly helped me get more of a grip on his view of the world.

According to Aleph, life is a pendulum in perpetual motion propelled by a life force. Our life experiences migrate between the two turning points to the left and to the right of centre, which marks the point where the pendulum stops when you die; the *death point*. The two arcs to the left and right of centre represent the depth of our experiences in life and are characterised as opposites – summer and winter, day and night, light and dark, hot and cold, male and female, strong and weak, love and hate, positive and negative, fire and water, dominant and submissive, aggressive and passive, hyper and hypo ... all the opposites.

The line separating the two arcs between the focal point and the *death point* represents our Goldilocks experiences – all good, all just right. In any given society, in terms of accepted social behaviour, that line represents the norm.

There is no norm, no line delineating sanity and insanity. At best, there is a desert mirage of a slippery ledge on the edge of those shifting sands. You become the person struggling to find a foothold there.

All this is what has brought me to my study and practice of *trample therapy*, which was inspired by Aleph's idea of a safer more humane coping support mechanism provided by professionals. It certainly worked for him, and it has worked for others so there must be something in it. At least he didn't try to deny he was a sick puppy. All I ever wanted to do was to be there for him; not be judgemental and narrow-minded and a know-all. He was the bullock pulling the load and I was the yoke that he needed to get the job done. I could never save him. I could never be Aleph. I would always be the 'blithe Spirit' in Shelley's poem; intangible and only in his imagination.

CHAPTER 12

Trample therapy gave me a lot to contemplate. Mental illness in my case was brought on by a combination of both mental and physical abuse that others in my early childhood and late teens perpetrated. For others, it could easily have been one or the other. Just as domestic violence could be either mental or physical abuse, mental illness too had its roots firmly planted in those toxic soils.

That toxicity often manifests itself as a blend of oppression and alienation boosted by neglect, hatred, jealousy, and often a desire for power and domination. For some there is sexual gratification as well. This behaviour destroys the victim's sense of net worth and self-esteem.

It is the same self-indulgent power-hungry, lustful maggot mentality that made me what I am; irretrievably flawed and on a never-ending downward spiral where little black sheep choke, are lost and forgotten.

Blithe Spirit's *trample therapy* made a lot of sense. Although I had been downtrodden and brutalised, Blithe Spirit's therapy offered an antidote devoid of any malice, fear or cruelty. It neutralised the poisons of past experiences embedded in my subconscious.

At the National Symposium on Mental Illness in Cannabia, Blithe Spirit further promoted her theory, justifying the therapy's benefits to long-term sufferers. There, in discussions with like-minded people and challenged by sceptics, she honed her theory to a point where she was granted permission to conduct a trial on its effectiveness on patients with a broad range of conditions. That's where I came in and provided the funding to set up a clinic for her to conduct research under laboratory conditions. Mostly, I wanted society to acknowledge and address the need for individuals to be able to be healed and rehabilitated.

There was more to Blithe Spirit's exotic 'trampling' techniques as well as some variations her colleagues employed which were rather risqué and involved an element of pain bordering on the erotic. One most positive outcome for the program was that people were lining up and paying good money to avail themselves of the therapy despite many of them having no history of mental illness. Go figure.

CHAPTER 13

Enticed by the political adventure afforded by a seat in that clipjoint they call the Parliament House of Umbugumbuland, I am now at a point where my main interest is focused on that pursuit.

In 1991, Umbugumbuland was finally granted provisional membership of the elite group of countries that had banded together to form The Alliance of the Heel of Achilles. Once a country was prepared to acknowledge its shortcomings, it was eligible to become a member of The Alliance, which brought with it special privileges in terms of trade, travel, taxation and security.

Umbugumbuland was slowly extricating itself from its insular diehard policies on immigration, racist views on superiority with covert enforcement of colour bars, arrogant attitudes towards its indigenous people, and intolerance towards other religious beliefs, languages and cultures. Its line in the sand as reactionary was beginning to fade as other political systems were treated with less disdain. Gender issues were also becoming a higher priority as they began to exert leverage on the outcome of various provincial and national polls. Only mental health issues languished in the catacombs of so called 'respite centres' with muted token references echoing out of the halls of academia, where government funding was squandered on the careers of politicians instead of focusing on the wellbeing of individuals.

That is some Achilles heel. It is no wonder that once Umbugumbuland had shown signs of progress in all these areas and was prepared to acknowledge it had a long way to go in addressing these shortcomings, that the international community softened its stance and granted the provisional membership. It meant that certain criteria had to be adhered to and benchmarks met before actual membership was granted.

Umbugumbuland's traditional trading partners and alliances had been cemented over five decades, and now a new generation of more liberally minded people with more *laissez-faire* attitudes was beginning to preside over a new-world order. Technology was sounding the death knell to the old guard, rendering them dinosaurs unwilling and/or unable to participate. Wealth and opportunity were the lures for the underprivileged to revolt against poverty, oppression, ideology and ignorance, and only an international alliance with a common goal could corral these benefits for the greater good.

After Umbugumbuland's admission, the global Alliance of the Heel of Achilles would be complete. A list of the member nations and their shortcomings follows:

- Woccowaccaland: A nation of racist wealthy exploitative warmongers
- West Blahblahland: Drug lords and irrational hotheads with short fuses
- East Blahblahland: Tribal warlords, witchdoctors and cannibals
- Suwajiland: A set of self-serving exploitative wealth management countries
- Allalalaland: Fanatical fundamentalists devoid of any reason
- Ellifafaland: A class-conscious stratified society
- North Lilulaland: Fear mongers and land grabbers
- Central Lilulaland: Overpopulated yet vacuous with no original thought
- South Lilulaland: Banana republic with monkey-see-monkey-do mentality
- East Lilulaland: Battleground zero where all wars are fought
- Umbugumbuland: Most of all the above, and poor mental health support.

Umbugumbuland's first task set by The Alliance was to develop economic ties with Central Lilulaland through educational exchanges and the development of sister-city relationships. Since Central Lilulaland was overpopulated yet vacuous with no original thought, Umbugumbuland had to come up with all the original ideas on how to set up educational exchanges and develop sister-city relationships.

Blithe Spirit was appointed to set up a think tank at Hoopla University as to the best way to address these goals and achieve desirable outcomes for both countries. Because most academics felt it would be impossible to operate in a vacuum where there was no original thought, they opted out, preferring to cruise along with whatever they were doing at Hoopla and forego the funding The Alliance was prepared to provide. Blithe Spirit, on the other hand, saw it as a wonderful opportunity to advance her *trample therapy* theory on patients devoid of any original thought.

Blithe Spirit led a group of twenty-eight Umbugumbuans from Hoopla University, including students and practitioners, to Sing Song University in Sing Song, an overpopulated city of 25 million people. At the same time, twenty-eight students and practitioners from Sing Song University were invited to attend Hoopla University. They wanted to do further research in creating false memories. Their studies so far were based on the premise that memories were stored with the formation of a protein in the brain. Each time a memory was recalled, the protein could be reformed or modified. How this process worked was a research question of great interest to neuroscientists.

The Central Lilulaland Government had an even

greater interest in the phenomenon. There was political advantage to be gained from understanding how false memories could be implanted covertly into the brains of citizens whose memories had been scarred by human rights violations in the past. Any hint of rebellion against the rule of government in Central Lilulaland was always met with brute force. In the previous year alone, a massive student demonstration against army rule resulted in thousands being massacred. The students would not yield. They were shot, crushed by tanks and heavy machinery, imprisoned and tortured.

Central Lilulaland had violated what was considered sacrosanct to the *raison d'être* of The Alliance of the Heel of Achilles – that every country should be prepared to acknowledge its own shortcomings. The only way for the government of Central Lilulaland to avoid this admission, which would cause great loss of face, was to deny that the massacre happened. So, if there was a way to transplant any memories of the event with false memories, the government wanted to know about it first.

False memories are sensory and emotional impressions blurred by imagination, belief, ambiguity and time. They can be affected by attitudes and beliefs. The government had to exploit this knowledge of the nature of false memories to create a negative evaluation of the event that would distort memory through the subconscious mind.

The research group concluded that it was

possible to get people to remember something that never happened if the implanted imaginary event was vivid enough. The scientific proof was in the chemistry of what was known as a 'memory trace'. The vividly imagined event could leave a memory trace in the brain that's like that of an experienced event.

The Sing Song University group wanted to gather empirical evidence to support their theories and to gain recognition by Hoopla University which was an internationally recognised university.

The only difficulty they encountered was getting anyone in Umbugumbuland to subject themselves to the severe image implant methods, or in other words, brainwashing. Consequently, they spent most of their time experimenting on one another. However, the severity of the image implanting was such that a human rights group had to intervene when several members of the group were rendered unconscious.

In the end, they simply made up the data and called it empirical, which was the closest thing to original thought they were ever going to get. Nobody else would have dared.

They were happy with that.

Meanwhile, at Sing Song University, Blithe Spirit had great difficulty getting volunteers for her therapy because she did not offer them the cultural gesture of free food, even though her therapy had nothing to do with being fed. Finally, they all agreed to let themselves be 'trampled' provided they were guaranteed that they would be fed at the end of each session. However, Blithe Spirit's team were disappointed with their results because all their volunteers were totally sane to start with and were only there for the food. Central Lilulalanders would lose face if they had to admit to outsiders that they had people who were insane or even mildly unbalanced in their community. They insisted that only criminals were insane, and criminals were usually executed or their organs harvested for transplants. Their state of mind was immaterial as brains for transplants were never taken from criminals.

***

That initial disaster wiped out any further university involvement in promoting academic and educational pursuits, and The Alliance went cold on exchange grants. However, as soon as issues like differing ideologies began to impact on the economic wellbeing of member countries, The Alliance became active again, supporting programs offering opportunities for the cross-fertilisation of ideas that might bring about a compromise.

Yeahwellah secured an invitation to participate at an Alliance symposium in Allalalaland. While they were all en route to Allalalaland, a small band of fanatical fundamentalists ran amok there, killing anyone whose ideology was based on a faith other than their own. Those actions soon escalated beyond control as splinter groups combined to launch a full-scale movement. High priests had recruited armies and secured funding, weapons and volunteers from several other countries within The Alliance.

According to one of The Alliance journalists who was sent to report on the outcomes of the symposium, everything went awry from the outset.

Instead of a warm welcome, a bunch of rebels hauled the journalist and all the international representatives including Yeahwellah out of the arrivals lounge of the Allalalaland airport and thrust them into a makeshift underground prison. They were tried as infidels and sentenced to be executed by decapitation. In shock, the journalist and the others all waited for ten days and eleven nights for the sentence to be carried out. Fortunately, they were all granted a reprieve when a Soothsayer in the Highest warned that the entire Alliance would self-destruct if the prisoners were not released forthwith.

After their release, when they were all being driven back to the airport to be deported, they saw children posing for photographs holding sub-machine guns and carrying human heads of so called infidels as trophies while their parents looked on. The women, all dressed in black, formed an outer circle, and gestured like witches, casting spells over a cauldron as the men herded them around with threats and commands. Craters gutted the roads and whole sections of the city had been reduced to rubble. Further on, a long line of men and some young boys, who looked about twelve to fifteen years old, were being beaten as they waited with eyes downcast contemplating their dilemma. Their hands were bound and many of them had gaping wounds with congealed blood. Directly ahead in a small clearing, the sound of machine gun fire lifted his line of sight to people falling like wheat stalks to the scythe.

Yeahwellah who was seated next to the journalist on the bus shuddered uncontrollably and began to panic. He kept voicing his thoughts out loudly, shouting that this was what *crazy* really looked like, sounded like, smelled like and felt like. Then he ran to the front of the bus, turned and addressed the representatives of all the other religions.

'As a representative of my country of Umbugumbuland I renounce my religion on the basis that religion is vying with the love of money as the root of all evil.'

He kept insisting he wanted out of this world forever and he wanted it fast.

'Sideswiped by the horror of all that has happened in the name of religion, I surrender my religious-spirit willingly.' He motioned towards the opened door of the bus. 'I can feel it being sucked out through that door right now. See!' He leaned outside of the door to the point where he might fall out. 'Already it is being shredded into spaghetti and forked into open mouths full of blood red teeth and blackened snake-like fangs.'

That was the point where the journalist felt Yeahwellah had lost it. He approached him cautiously and helped him back to his seat where Yeahwellah just froze and kept staring at the roof of the bus. Although they all received counselling when they arrived at the airport prior to their departure to their respective countries, it had no effect on Yeahwellah. He remained curled up in a foetal position on the floor in one corner of the airport lounge.

I have no knowledge of when Yeahwellah returned from Allalalaland. Somehow he had simply vanished. It was quite a few days after The Alliance journalist's article that Blithe Spirit finally tracked him down to an attic in an abandoned church on the outskirts of Waking. There she found my shadow; a mound of flesh huddled in a corner beneath one of the huge roughly-hewn oak beams. Fused tightly to the palm of his hand was a little round glass bowl the size of a macadamia nut with a small hole cut out of the top. Protruding from the bowl through his clenched fingers, she recognised the eight-millimetre hollowed-out glass stem or 'straight shooter' of a crack pipe. Although it was the tool of choice for smoking crack cocaine or crystal meth, she knew immediately that the dope Yeahwellah had smoked was far more powerful when she saw the remnants of the orange, crystalline, ear-waxy substance in the clear plastic packet beside him.

I can understand why he chose it. It was the only dope that had never failed me; that could take away the greatest pain in the shortest time. It was DMT; formula $C_{12} H_{16} N_2$, known as dimethyltryptamine or 'Dream Time'.

How could I forget it? You would hold the pipe and roll it slightly around and about, up and down so as not to allow the DMT to burn black when you applied the flame to the base of the bowl. As the vapours began to rise, you would suck on the stem extremely slowly before your whole world exploded within your head.

The effect, though short, is intense and with a rapid onset. Euphoria sets in and your mind loses all sense of reality. You spin into a new dimension with a full kit of colours smothering and intoxicating you. It is as if someone hot-wired all your senses simultaneously. The mind becomes caught up in an infinite feedback loop where it begins looking at itself, looking at itself, looking at itself, like an image reflected in a mirror, in a mirror, in a mirror.

As a hallucinogen, the effect is not unlike magic mushrooms or LSD, but maxed out. With DMT, you cannot imagine a stranger drug or stranger experience; it is classified as the most powerful hallucinogen known to man and science. It raises all kinds of issues like what is reality and what is three-dimensional space and time. On the first toke, there is a sense of all the air in the room being sucked out. On the second toke, colours begin racing together into a mandala of floral, slowly rotating orange-yellow lava-like life forms. With the third toke, there is the crackling sound of flame followed by a series of tunnels or chambers that you are tumbling down. The place or space that you burst into is like an underground dome full of ricocheting geometric hallucinations – an astral voyage into consciousness.

For Yeahwellah, it would have been like an icicle through the brain that melted slowly away and left no traces of those memories of Allalalaland, or anything else.

It was all over at last.

No, it wasn't!

CHAPTER 14

If you want my opinion as Aleph's psychologist, Yeahwellah's trip to Allalalaland as it panned out was an unmitigated disaster. Aleph needed the ideological checks and balances Yeahwellah provided when he was flying high with his entrepreneurial flair. He stopped Aleph flying too close to the sun and getting burned. Yeahwellah was his keeper as well as his safety net.

Aleph only had himself to blame for Yeahwellah's demise because it was he who suggested the trip. Yeahwellah could have stayed home safe and sound in his little faith cocoon and nothing like this would have happened. On the other hand, we all must put our beliefs to the test to see how they stack up against those of others. We all must live with the consequences when we step up to the plate. Yeahwellah lost his faith. Aleph learned a lesson. Hopefully it will stand him in good stead with his politicking. Religion and politics; stab or be stabbed.

Yeahwellah left me a note, and Aleph needs to know what was in the note as I believe it could help give him some form of closure. I am enclosing it in his diary so that he can deal with it privately. He will deal with it. Aleph always does. He sucks up all his sorrows and locks them up in the darkest corner of his brain and reasons that when there is no more space, then all the darkness will be gone. Aleph has this ability to turn every negative into a positive and that is the key to his survival.

Dear Blithe,

What a mug I was to think Aleph was a modern-day Moses and that I might be Jesus and that together we might bring love and peace to the world doing God's work. Of all the religions I have ever known or heard about, no two were ever the same, and deep down they all hated each other. I believe now that religion was never about God. It has always been about Man and a means to a selfish end. What I witnessed in Allalalaland caused me to surrender my faith and I have no regrets.

All these years, I have put up with Aleph's hair-brained schemes and his Midas touch, but man, did he miss the boat when it came to realising that life was no more than a soap bubble; perfect one moment and popped the next. Now, how bright does a person have to be to work that out?

To Aleph I say this:

I'm not sorry it had to end this way. Think of

Christ dying on the cross. In the end, there was so much to be learned from it all. That is my sacrifice for you. By the time you read this, I will have arrived at the end of my rainbow. Talk about going out in peace. Man, the hippies had it all worked out.

I could have done it your way, Aleph, and hung in there with my dick in one hand and a Bible in the other. Instead, I succumbed to the tangible experiences of the Dream Time.

You're on your own Aleph. Do you hear me? Try saying 'Fuck you!' to the system with your politicking and your money-making ventures because religion certainly doesn't work. See what sort of a shitstorm you can conjure up this time.

To you, to Blithe and to Scupper, I say
Adios Amigos!

CHAPTER 15

To help me get over the shock loss of Yeahwellah, Blithe suggested during one of her *trampling therapy* sessions on me that I take up an offer from the Hoopla Community Council to participate in a goodwill tour of Woccowaccaland that The Alliance was prepared to subsidise on a dollar-for-dollar basis. The council trumpeted my expertise in land reclamation techniques used on the golf course and the international airport and the canal residential developments, and included an outline of my innovative program promoting wetland conservation and methods of rebalancing environments under stress. As well, the community council went to great lengths to point out to The Alliance that one of the council's representatives had unparalleled performance credentials in the stock market investment related category of equity derivatives trading, which was a relatively recent phenomenon in both Umbugumbuland

and overseas. I believe that was the one that ultimately clinched the deal for the council.

They did not mention that it was the same person – me alone – that had all those skills. This enabled the council chairman (who had no expertise whatsoever) to freeload on my credentials. In fact, the third delegate, the deputy mayor of Hoopla City, had no special credentials either, other than being a deputy. I suggested to the council that the deputy mayor's signature could be useful if we needed to set up a sister-city relationship with one of the Woccowaccaland cities, and that's what got him his place on this junket.

I had heard about Woccowaccaland as the 'land of the free and easy' and was looking forward to going there to ascertain firsthand what their idea of the phrase 'free and easy' encompassed. After all, as a country mired in the slave trade for centuries, surely they had figured it out. I was in full political apprenticeship mode and I needed to focus on someone with credentials and expertise upon which to develop my political mindset.

The second thing that Woccowaccaland was notorious for was its business acumen. I was keen to hone my own management skills in business and hoped I could learn from them. Woccowaccaland had set up and managed slaughterhouses in almost every country except Umbugumbuland. Those people were so good at running the business of slaughtering that they could derive huge profits even from slaughter yards in other countries where they had no visible presence.

After arriving at the international airport in Yeee Haaa, Woccowaccaland, the three of us were all taken aside and individually interrogated as a security precaution. My room was pitch dark except for a reading lamp placed so close to my face that I could feel the heat radiating from it. It was impossible to work out who else was in the room, but I would have recognised the voices of the other delegates if they had been in the same room as me. At first, the Woccowaccans couldn't decide whether I spoke English or not. Eventually, they agreed that it was a variation of their own language and figured it was essentially a pidgin English or an English-based creole language.

They wanted to know about my social values, my political persuasion and my religious beliefs. I was asked to give examples of my stereotypes of coloured people, disabled people, mentally impaired people, dwarfs and terrorists. It was as if they were trying to trick me into saying something they wanted to hear. Finally, I had to list five firm prejudices I held before my passport was stamped and I could enter the country.

As it turned out, it was a lot worse for the other two delegates. They were not allowed to enter the country and were mistakenly deported to South Lilulaland where they were placed in indefinite detention pending an inquiry into where they had come from and whether they posed a threat to national security. Then, because it involved matters of national security, they lost all their rights of *habeas corpus* and simply disappeared.

I only heard about all this after I returned to Umbugumbuland.

Rewind to my being accepted into the country. My status went from being treated like a suspected felon to an honoured guest. That was until the three delegates from Alliance member countries found out I was from Umbugumbuland. When it came to sharing a cab to our hotel next to the convention centre in downtown Yeee Haaa, they came up with some lame excuse about people from provisional membership countries having to ride in P-plated vehicles. But when one of them read on my bio on the guest list that I was a specialist in derivatives trading, they suddenly wanted to travel with me in my P-plated vehicle.

They lived to regret that decision. We were travelling through one of the low socio-economic areas that the driver referred to as a 'ghetto' when our cab was hijacked and we were all mugged, including the driver. Our cab was stolen along with our money, and we were left bleeding on the side of the roadway. Eventually, a group of dreadlocked creatures that looked like they had been dredged out of the nearby lagoon, came to our aid and invited us into their squats which had no electricity, sanitation or running water. They claimed Woccowaccaland had been plunged into a deep economic crisis and they had all lost their jobs, homes and life savings. They had no choice but to scrounge around and plunder what they could from 'zombie' suburbs where the abandoned properties had a net value equal to the amount of scrap metal that could be dug out of the walls, windows, roofs and under sinks and around toilet cisterns.

I was shocked because I had always believed Woccowaccaland to be a land of great wealth, innovation and perpetual wonder, where anything the people wanted or dreamed about could be brought to fruition by endeavour or simply bought with cash or favour. The other reason I came here and wasn't going to tell you about is that I hoped I might 'purchase' a certificate of mental health from one of their leading institutions. This would put me in the top ten percentile of the population back in Umbugumbuland. It could prove to be invaluable in safeguarding my political career when I finally embarked upon it, which was going to be soon.

Well, I can tell you now I certainly misjudged the Woccowaccan dream and soon abandoned my quest for a sanity certificate from that country. The banks were broke. As for innovation, the people were too busy reinventing the hurricane lamp for lighting and burning sump-oil for fuel. As for perpetual wonder, the only thing they wondered about was where their next meal was coming from. There were no dreams, only nightmares with droves of desperate people ending up in prison. At least a prison term got them a square meal and a roof over their heads and protection from thugs.

Soon after, word had filtered through to the authorities that four overseas delegates had been ambushed in the ghetto. A cordon of riot squad police was dispatched on a search and rescue mission, and our squat was soon surrounded by hordes of little men in black armour waving shields and truncheons and running around like black ants out of an anthill that had been doused in kerosene and set on fire. Our hosts were warned not to resist before they were set upon with rubber truncheons and steel batons, then tasered and trussed up like chilled chickens in the cooler section of a supermarket. Despite our protestations on their behalf, those apprehended knew the drill and within minutes were prepared to confess to anything rather than sustain the savage beatings being meted out by the riot police.

We were whisked away and before long found ourselves being pampered in the foyer of the Hotel Colossus next door to the convention centre in Yeee Haaa. This was no ordinary hotel. This was one of only two hotels in the nation to have received a double Black Stump Seven-Star rating for both the hotel and its restaurant. Better still, it had been awarded this distinction for six years in a row. Anyone who knew anything about hospitality had to learn it from this mob.

At first, I couldn't wait to get out of there. This place had nothing to offer me and there was no way I was going to indulge in the fantasies of such a privileged country that treated its citizens so badly. Our 'crazies' were treated far better than those guys out in that squat back in the ghetto. In fact, I was going to take the first opportunity to tell these god-forsaken people what I thought of their human rights shortcomings and that they should go back to the end of the queue, hang their head in shame and reapply for their membership of The Alliance of the Heel of Achilles after they sorted out those shortcomings. What a joke. These guys had no sense of right and wrong; they walked around in blinkers, devoid of empathy. They were a permanent threat to the safety of anyone who was underprivileged. They were cold, calculating, egocentric, ethnocentric neo-megalomaniacs and they had the hide to call others 'crazies'.

Anyhow, I never got to deliver my lecture on derivatives trading. The speaker appointed to talk before me introduced what he called 'a new wave of economic thought that rendered everything else in the derivatives genre as passé'. The truth was that it did do exactly that, so I skipped my bit on derivative trading and focused instead on my land reclamation act and my wetlands and environmental conservation and rehabilitation gig.

The 'new wave of economic thought' lecture was the first example I had of the edge that Woccowaccaland had over the rest of the world as a place of great wealth, innovation and perpetual wonder; where anything the people wanted or dreamed about could be brought to fruition.

His talk introduced a concept known as CFDs – Contracts for Differences. They had not even been invented in Umbugumbuland. A contract for differences is an arrangement, a contract between a client and a broker, whereby differences in settlement are made through cash payments rather than by the delivery of physical goods or securities. So, you don't need to own a security to buy or sell it. All you have to do is tender a slender 2% margin and open an account for as little as $1000 to become eligible to trade with millionaires and high rollers. The great advantage of this type of trading over the *passé* strategies I had employed in my derivatives trading in Umbugumbuland, is that the CFD owner receives cash dividends and participates in stock splits which increase the trader's return on investment.

That was how these desperadoes in Woccowaccaland, who were still reeling under the double whammy of their debt crisis and a commodity price collapse, had managed to leapfrog their cash constraints and remain in the big league. It meant that CFDs in stocks, indexes, treasuries, currencies, commodities and sector CFDs could be applied nationally as well as in markets worldwide.

So, instead of the Woccowaccan trip helping me come to terms with the loss of Yeahwellah, it yielded me a net gain of setting up my own broking house in every capital city of Umbugumbuland. McNaught Securities Trading Company Limited was appointed as an agent with exclusive rights to trading CFDs nationally and internationally. It was a licence to print money. For the trader, there was no borrowing or shorting costs. There were few or no fees charged for trading a CFD and the broker made money on every deal from the trader, paying the 'spread' which was the difference between the bid and ask price that the market-maker offered.

Ironically, I half found myself rejoicing that Yeahwellah was out of my life. He had become too much of a burden on my psyche. Religion had hounded me all my life. From those days when I became inextricably intertwined and fucked in the head by my stepfather's religious sect, to Yeahwellah's ranting and ravings that left so many questions unanswered, I needed to step back and reconsider my position as I wrestled with my God. I needed religion to remain dead forever with Yeahwellah.

I realised there was no place for it in my life anymore – I mean religion where man assumes the role of God and plays god in God's name. I mean religion that claims to exist through a divine right yet glorifies war and gorges itself on the spoils of war. The word of God might as well have been written in Urdu or in Hindi, judging by the way it has been diced, sliced, turned, toasted, burned, roasted and dished up as God's laws that have no resemblance to the English version I had unearthed in my readings of the Bible. No, religion is just a tool in man's quest for absolute power, and if any other religion poses a threat to that power, it must be destroyed. Religion is a curse. I want none of it.

Instead, I chose to live by faith alone where God is not everything good, but where everything good is God. To those who wank on about being prepared to die for their religion, I wish them God speed and rest my case.

To rehabilitate my psyche, I decided to aspire to a future greatness and not a former pursuit, because there was no greatness in my former self. I must 'detox' and expunge the religiosity from my life and allow my psyche to be sustained through faith alone. The meddling of mortals with the scriptures seeks to control until it becomes a religion, and it is the religion, not the faith, that triumphs over all. That is religion with its built-in laws to subdue the true believers who expose the leaders for what they are; religion with its built-in scarecrows to deter sceptics; religion with its threats of fire and damnation in Hell and banishment from the kingdom of God. This had no more calling for me.

Vale Yeahwellah. Though you served me well, I need to recalibrate and follow my faith. Wherever you are, feel free to pass that message on to Hosanna in the Highest.

CHAPTER 16

Having finally decided to separate myself from the Church, I was moved to further explore my newfound interest in the power of the State. After all, they worked in tandem on so many fronts – pursuit of power-hungry goals, greed for money, lies, corruption, deceit, fear mongering, false promises, brainwashing, and extortion through tithe or taxation for nothing in return.

Blithe was again the one to encourage me because *trampling therapy* had become common practice, with variations to the theory proving to be enervating and the practice too exhausting. I also suspected she was bored and was searching for a taste of the power that might emanate from political ascendancy. She knew that I could do anything if I set my mind to it. There was a touch of finesse in politics that fast-tracked the pleasure of power directly to the brain without it being filtered through the extremities of the body. Yes, there was evidence of this desire despite her masked pretence at not hearing my twice repeated suggestion that she would make a fine First Lady and the firm whip hand behind me as president of Umbugumbuland. She sneezed on both occasions. When you have worked out what that means, you will know you are on the same plane as me.

Crazies don't miss a trick, but don't take that as a suggestion that I might be crazy. It's just that I know a lot about how crazies think, just like I know a lot about how religious people think, and how millionaires think, and how mathematicians think, and all the other madmen around who think they are sane and that everyone else is crazy. Even Blithe might be crazy; they say psychologists usually are. I mean, who could propose such a dumb-arse theory like *trample therapy* theory and make any claim to sanity? Only a psychologist, ... or a psychiatrist; equal chance.

Now, compare them to someone like me who is continually proving himself a winner in an intellectual as well as economic capacity, and every other element of human endeavour that I put my efforts into. No chance, fire ants!

Continuing my 'apprenticeship', I decided to go to East Blahblahland because the politics there operated at a level that was only a notch or two above the ape population and I wanted to start off at the lowest level of human endeavour for social control. That might sound racist, but that's me; I'm not perfect. At the helm were tribal warlords, witchdoctors and cannibals.

I paid for the trip myself this time because I could afford it and I could not stand the interference of the chain of command under The Alliance. To my surprise I could see from the moment I arrived in East Blahblahland that the country was making millions of tourist dollars out of overseas horror seekers who never even left the airport. They paid their money to watch through bulletproof glass panes as hundreds of purple people were tried, convicted, then mutilated and cannibalised simply because of their colour or because of their tribal affiliation. The tourists bought souvenir clubs and machetes like those used in the peepshow, or articles of witchery or a shrunken head before catching the next plane out.

I was told, after making further enquiries about the phenomenon, that every now and then, with the ascendancy of another warlord to power, the political fortunes of the people would turn and the orange people (formally the oppressors) were herded into holding pens and mutilated and cannibalised in return. It was only then that I noticed many of the purple and orange people, including drivers, porters, cleaners, office staff, public servants and even children of all ages with limbs missing.

How was it that this country had been granted membership of The Alliance while Umbugumbuland waited all that time just to gain provisional membership? Apparently, when the matter was raised at Alliance headquarters in Woccowaccaland, the response was that The Alliance did not concern itself with traditional matters as that would impinge on the cultural sovereignty of the member nations.

The next country I visited on my fact-finding mission was on the second lowest rung of the ladder of social control. West Blahblahland was a nation of drug lords and irrational hot-headed gang and community leaders who often took the law into their own hands when confronted with backlogs in dealing with problems of law enforcement and especially for unpaid debts. In one city, the lord mayor often joined vigilante gangs headed by past acquaintances and childhood friends to shoot drug traffickers and any other undesirables in cold blood. The biggest problem for the government was when rival drug lords clashed over territory, or there was infighting and the funds those drug lords provided to run the country dried up. The solution was to remove the president and replace him or her with a new president that the dominant drug lord appointed.

On the third lowest rung was a banana republic with a monkey-see-monkey-do mentality called South Lilulaland. There, the people even looked like monkeys. They all dressed in jungle greens so that the moment they walked anywhere near a rainforest, they vanished in camouflage. It was hard to work out who was in charge and who was not because they all looked alike. The jungle was in the background most of the time so the place always looked deserted. That was until there was any suggestion of food, and then the forest moved to the food source.

One evidence of social control was when someone spat out something on the ground. That enabled me to recognise the law enforcers who suddenly materialised out of the jungle, pounced on the spitter and dissolved back into the jungle with them. When I went over to examine the spat object by touching it with my shoe, I found that it stuck to it like glue and could not be removed. It upset me so much I almost wished he would be given more than a reprimand and even a small fine for the inconvenience he had caused me. I was told that the substance was gum from the sap of a tree and that on the second offence, the person would be punished with fifty strokes of the cane to his bare back. I thought, *Shit, that was pretty serious stuff* and left the country with only that on my mind. I figured there wasn't much I was going to be able to glean about a government that would appeal to any of the blokes back home.

In East Lilulalaland, I faced another dilemma trying to liaise with government officials on setting up some kind of diplomatic relationship. The country was often referred to as Battleground Zero where all wars were fought. Because the country was always in a state of war, it was hard to work out who was in control, and even then, they were always suspicious that you might be a spy and better off in detention until the end of the war, which could be never. As soon as I heard that, I was out of there like you wouldn't believe, but not before I bought some hooch which was why my English had deteriorated so much in this diary note extract about my trip there. In fact, if they had caught me, I could have been imprisoned or even executed. So, I gave it to a Woccowaccan who said he didn't care whether he was imprisoned or even executed because there was an economic crisis back home and he had nothing to go back to. I watched him, and before losing sight of him, saw him sell it to a local who on-sold it to someone else who on-sold it again. It seemed to me that as a currency, marijuana might be a part answer to our problem with counterfeit notes in Umbugumbuland. I made a diary note of that idea.

North Lilulaland was nothing like any of the other Lilulalands. They were a different race who dressed like people who had been carved out of stone. I tried to imagine how they could get into cars or even buses, much less work in the fields or make love anywhere other than in the bedroom after chiselling off their garments.

The architecture was extravagant. Each city looked like a fairyland with its beautiful buildings. I was confident I could learn a lot about government from these people and was keen to make some contacts. Everywhere I went people plied me with this colourless liquid that exploded in my brain as I thrust back each shot into my throat. I had thrown back about fifteen of those shots by the time I met the head honcho, and could not focus on the guy's face enough to have even a faint hope of recognising him in the morning. Fortunately, he was totally blotto as well from meeting important people all day.

He decided to take me home to 'discuss matters further' and meet his wife. I had to agree as I had no idea where I was. Also, I was just getting to like that rocket fuel and simply had to find out why he wanted me to meet his wife.

Well, I found out soon enough and it wasn't because he wanted me to seduce her or anything like that. He brought me home because he thought she would spare him a beating for coming home drunk if he brought home a foreigner. I can tell you it made no difference whatsoever. I had never seen a man so brutally beaten and so relentlessly; there was no way I could do anything to help him. She was built like a public telephone box. I guessed his stone clothing would give him some protection but after more than half an hour of beating, when she took a broom to him, I had my doubts whether this man was going to live long enough to be my contact in North Lilulaland.

The strangest thing was that next morning she became the sweetest thing imaginable, if you could imagine a public telephone box looking like the sweetest thing imaginable. He was sitting at the kitchen table looking fresh and clean in his singlet and shorts as she went around all the bruises over his body, dabbing them with a wet cloth and rubbing them with salve. She brought him tea and served him sausages and egg, and when he snapped his fingers and pointed at me, she did the same for me, nodding and bowing to me with every move she made towards me. She brought in his clothes, which had been warmed beside the wood stove, and after he had finished his breakfast, slid a freshly ironed shirt over his singlet, and the coat over his freshly ironed shirt. She brushed down his coat as he put on his long trousers, and put on his shoes, tied his laces and applied the final touch of delicate spittle with a short shoe shine on the top of both shoes. Go figure!

I called him 'Dumbo' because I knew he would never work out what it really meant. I told him he was going to be my man and that if he joined forces with me he could hire a bodyguard of at least five beautiful women to protect him from the phone box and help him to live happily ever after when she wasn't around. He laughed and his eyes developed a sparkle that reignited every time he saw me and recalled what I had offered him. Yep, he was going to be my man in North Lilulaland and I was going to own him.

On the final leg of my tour, Blithe met up with me in Ellifafaland. She was fascinated at all she had read about belly dancers in this the belly dancer capital of the world. She was so captivated, we just watched belly dancers all day every day. That meant my potential contacts from Ellifafaland had to watch belly dancers too, but they didn't seem to mind. In fact, I got the feeling that they appreciated my special attention to that art form and it enhanced my standing with them.

Everyone I spoke to in Ellifafaland was most enthusiastic about the idea of Umbugumbuland becoming a member of The Alliance, and they kept offering up possible ways of doing business together. However, it was never country to country; all the proposals were individual to individual. That explained the wealth embedded in their rings, bangles, earrings and necklaces of gold, silver and precious coloured stones. At first, I was so impressed with the nobility of these people. They were best described as simpatico and the women were stunningly beautiful with big round brown eyes and long silken hair. They were tall, slim and elegant and I couldn't help wanting to capture the rhythm of their stride in verse.

It was when someone invited us to visit a jewellery factory that all my pleasant thoughts about these people went sour. I knew with one look at the emaciated elf-like craftsmen, women and children slaving at their tables with downcast eyes, obviously afraid to engage in eye contact with their 'masters', that this was a very class-conscious stratified society. It was as if my excitement about these people suddenly went from orgasmic to cataclysmic. I was done, I felt violated just being in the presence of such arrogance and disrespect for human life. I wondered how a government that supported such a system could possibly be tolerated in the twenty-first century. I wanted no more to do with them. The Alliance of the Heel of Achilles had a lot to answer for.

Most certainly, Umbugumbuland had shortcomings of its own but none as bad as what I had seen in those member countries. I figured that must have been why we had been excluded for so long.

After I returned, I decided to give a presentation at Hoopla University to some delegates from The Alliance who were visiting Umbugumbuland as part of the provisional membership process. I couched it in such a way that would allow them to go away and think about it, hoping the messages would filter through as would the benefits of reviewing their own shortcomings from an Umbugumban standpoint. I chose to speak on religion as an example.

Religion, according to The Alliance, was classified in terms of sets of beliefs. I outlined how each set could be reclassified into sub-sets. Therefore, in terms of their cardinality, I figured that their hierarchical standing could be determined by applying the mathematics of the *Continuum Hypothesis* which I renamed the *Infinitus Hypothesis.* My presentation was constructed and summarised on the whiteboard, and a handout made available to all the delegates. It addressed the three sets of religious beliefs that The Alliance had stipulated as universal and all encompassing, and I based my argument on the following premise in the handout:

- S1 represents the in-sect religions that can, have and always will be divided. It is monotheistic, extreme and dangerous.

- S2 represents the other-sect religion that tolerates no fractional parts. It too is monotheistic, extreme and dangerous.
- S3 represents the non-sect bongo drum and clang of metal metaphysical and magical religions. It includes the viewpoints of academics, atheists and agnostics. It is passive and upholds peace as the equilibrium that all religions aspire to.
- Consider S1, S2 and S3 as examples of infinite sets.

I followed this with a series of dot points stating:

- Because S2 with no fractional parts is a subset of S1, which can, has and always will be divided, then the cardinality of S1 > the cardinality of S2.
- Because S1 is a subset of S3, if peace is the equilibrium that all religions aspire to, then the cardinality of S3 > the cardinality of S1.
- Therefore, the cardinality of S2 must be < the cardinality of S3.
- Applying the *Infinitus Hypothesis*: as S3 for non-sects has minimal possible cardinality, then the cardinality for S1 being in-sects and expressed as 2 to the power of aleph-naught is > the cardinality of S2 for other-sects expressed as aleph-naught and the cardinality of S3 for non-sects > the cardinality of S1 for in-sects.

In summary, I concluded that:

- Therefore, there is no set S for which: aleph-naught < S < 2 to the power of aleph-naught

- <u>So,</u> there is a smaller cardinal number aleph-one which is > aleph-naught
- and 2 to the power aleph-naught = aleph-one.

The end.

I was then escorted back to my padded cell, injected with a pacifier and woke up in a straitjacket. See what can happen when you get ahead of yourself?

Thank God that was only a dream, although I could never be sure if it was. Apparently, according to Blithe, that whole scenario was just a figment of my imagination on one of those planes I told you about where I succumbed to psychosis brought on by past experiences of experimenting with hallucinogenic drugs like DMT and magic mushrooms and toad-skin soup. In fact, I was so sure it really happened that I was beginning to have doubts about the veracity of Blithe's statements and whether she could be trusted anymore. I even wondered if it was better that she should be out of my life. Maybe she had outlived her usefulness and was out to get me.

That might sound strange coming from my lips, but I was beginning to take a firm view on the validity of conspiracy theories; the *Eye of Providence*, the secret handshakes, dumbing-down chemicals in the water supply, communications monitoring, genetic engineering, the implications ensconced in the internet of things, happenings for economic convenience, covert agendas within The Alliance, warmongering for profit, and the demonisation of contrarian thinkers and whistle blowers. Too many people had an economic or political interest in maintaining the status quo.

My dream of wanting to make Umbugumbuland great was never going to happen by maintaining the status quo or kowtowing to The Alliance. It was time to take a shot at entering the corridors of power. It was time to break down the barriers to progress and build a better, fairer world.

CHAPTER 17

Knock, knock.

This is where I ask you to come into my world … if you're game. I say game, because in my world it never gets any filthier than politics. Just attaching yourself to me like Yeahwellah did religiously and Blithe did psychologically and Scupper did economically is a big ask. When I say it's about politics, this time that involves a mammoth lifestyle change. It's like being asked to abandon your afternoon bicycle ride to the corner store in exchange for a once in a lifetime space travel adventure to another planet. It'll be like one of those mystery flights the airlines offer. You don't get to know where you're going until you get off the plane.

At this point in the story, you can still opt out and go back to what you believed in before this offer. Alternatively, you can just push the door open a little and take a peek. So long as you keep one foot outside, you can always back out. Think of it as a love affair. Until you commit to love in a love affair, it's not love, it's an affair; a fantasy. Fantasies are one thing, but a love affair; that's deep shit.

So, are you coming in or staying out? You know the story so far. If you decide to come in, you get to be a gatekeeper of one of the doors to *Aleph's World of Absurd Political Thought*, which will lay the foundations of a new way of life for all Umbugumbuans.

If you're staying out, just shut the book and ask for your money back. Good luck with that last bit. Ha! Ha! You can't even score a free lunch these days much less get your money back on a book that you don't even get to read.

That's absurd!

Warning! Yeahwellah got burned.

CHAPTER 18

The door's ajar. Inside, it's dark. To find the light switch, you can place your face against the outside wall, reach in, stretch and fumble around a bit and do hand sweeps up and down the inside wall. Eventually you'll work out the switch is out of reach.

You must come right in to get to the switch.

You didn't really believe you could peek into Aleph's World and then back out, did you? That's naive. Where's the commitment in that? Or do you just want to frolic in the park with your sweetheart all day, knowing that without committing, you can still return to your safe little nest at dusk and pretend it never happened? Politics must be a love affair that you are committed to.

If you decide to come in, I can promise you one thing. The moment you flick on that switch, it's like being born again. I don't mean the religious born-again shit but a 'seeing-the-light' born again. That's where you get to find out the truth about the state that Umbugumbuans are in. Seeing-the-light is about finding another way that can be so exhilarating that you could lose control.

I want to be up front with you. This love affair may fuck with your head.

If in doubt, stay out. Shut the book!

CHAPTER 19

If you're reading this, you've opted in and committed yourself to developing a passion for politics. Everyone needs to develop a passion for politics. People need to take responsibility for the politics and the politicians that control their lives. That's why they say you get the politicians you deserve. If you think you deserve better, then insist upon it. Don't whinge. Get involved. Don't expect the rest of the world to feel sorry for you because you're being ripped off, exploited, trampled, chewed up, sucked dry and spat out.

That's why I decided I'm going to do something about it. But be meticulous. That's how I got to be so successful and made all that money. Sure, there was a bit of luck but it wasn't the sort of luck where you suddenly get hit with the 'luck stick'. No, I made my own luck. I put a lot of thought and work into achieving my success, and I have been doing the same developing my political mindset.

You all know what a fun park is. Well, the world of politics is just one big theme park where all the politicians are having all the fun and making all the money. You and I and the rest of the crowd are the mugs being asked at the gate not to bring food and drink into the park so they can charge us twice the price inside. You and I and the rest of the crowd are the suckers waiting in line inside the park to be 'taken for a ride' on The Roll and Toaster or frightened shitless on The Cloak and Dagger Train or The Shower of Terror. Need I say more?

Central to the theme park is the monumental 'Palace of Power' symbolising the wealth and power of the government of Umbugumbuland and aptly named The Clipjoint. The Clipjoint is the seat of government building where they make all the rules that determine whether we prosper or whether we wither on the vine. Mostly it's the latter, hence the name.

When you go to visit the place, they voodoo you with x-rays, metal-detect you and get sniffer dogs to check you out before they take you up and down the elevator until they think it's safe to let you out and lock you in 'The Gallery'. From The Gallery, you get to experience the goings on in 'The Yodelling Chamber'. The Yodelling Chamber is where members of government and the opposition shout at each other across the chasm that separates their ideologies. Their utterances ricochet from wall to wall and eventually reach the visitors in The Gallery as an echo which makes no sense whatsoever. It's like wearing a hearing aid, with several people around you all talking simultaneously, the music blasting and several semitrailers outside thundering down an incline with the airbrakes screaming bloody murder.

Well, at the next election, you and I are going to waltz into the Palace of Power simply by convincing the people to exercise their right to vote. We will beat the politicians at their own game and smash the polls and appoint the politicians we deserve.

In our struggle for a new and improved democracy, I bid you welcome as 'The Gatekeepers' and I name you 'Thee'.

CHAPTER 20

Aleph's Army for Armageddon is the new people's party that will govern Umbugumbuland. Scupper, Blithe and you, Thee, will be responsible for the party mechanism, and I shall lead it. Scupper represents the rich, Blithe the poor, and you, Thee, represent the masses from the individual and the group right through to the community, state-wide and nationally. Everyone else in the party will share in the joy brought about by an apocalypse that will eradicate the politics of corrupt and dysfunctional government. Through you, Thee, the people become the government, the rule of law, the guardians of peace and order, and the sole beneficiaries of our country's prosperity.

We must be forever watchful of the powerful, and equally so of the disenfranchised. As well, we must never underestimate the influence of the silent majority within the broader community. You must commit yourself to this love affair with the people of

Umbugumbuland. That is how we will make her great. The Alliance of the Heel of Achilles will learn from us.

Because of your apathy for politics in the past, I shall be the one who determines the policies and the strategies for the party going into the election. You three will organise the party and implement those strategies. From day one, the AAA Party brand name will be triple-A rated in terms of its performance standards. The AAA Party brand name will be our guarantee to the electorate that we will keep our promises. It will appear on billboards on every highway, on business shopfronts in every street, on every form of clothing by every fashion house, and stamped clearly upon every act of government in the future.

Our slogan will be:

Vote AAA: We Offer You Nothing.
We Keep Our Promises!

You see Thee, they say in politics that you get what you deserve. So, if the AAA Party offers nothing, it's because it's what you deserve. The party needs to be told what the people really want from government; not the other way around where the government tells the people what they want. Government isn't a childcare centre. Ask for what you want. Insist on it. These needs will then be addressed as AAA Party policy. Once the policy carries the AAA Party brand name, it becomes your guarantee that it will happen because the AAA Party keeps its promises. That's the rationale behind our slogan.

When the people realise they are voting for what they really want and what they deserve, the AAA Party will be a force to reckon with. We must hammer home that a vote for Aleph's Army for Armageddon is a vote for what they want from government.

Sometimes, even when you tell people outright that they are being gypped, they don't want to believe it. It becomes an affront to their intelligence. Maybe they don't want to be hurt by hearing the truth. Maybe they would rather deny the lie and feel the pain before they are prepared to accept it. Some would rather continue to suffer rather than deny the lie. That's textbook self-harm through political fallout.

If we remain up front with the electorate, voters will realise that government is always about being gypped in one way or another. The AAA Party sets itself apart from the opposition − that bad bunch of legitimate racketeers. We offer the best value for your vote.

Let me tell you a story. When they had the big change of name celebration for the Hoopla Hospital Mental Ward in the sixties, I was there playing games with the shrinks and breaking windows to get their attention and respect. The event was supposed to be quite a momentous one. A change of name to Hoopla Hospital Respite Centre reflected a change of attitudes heralded by social scientists in the press as 'an awakening to the plight of the forgotten people'. The local Member of Parliament reminded us on the day by using the same words, because all politicians loved using euphemisms when they didn't really believe what they were saying.

The entire wing was packed with politicians, social workers, medical professionals, family members and people from all walks of life, from the homeless to the rich and famous. They all clapped after the MP's speech, except for the inmates, so it makes you wonder who the mentally impaired people really were.

The hospital board thought the event would provide a wonderful opportunity to raise funds from the public so the wing was asked to organise a fete of sorts to be held in the outside courtyard. The offer of support from local businesses was quite remarkable, and the organisers were flooded with tents, umbrellas and several marquees all boasting their product names and contact details.

For a set fee, the usual weekend marketeers were invited to fill the stalls with their wares. Paintings and handicrafts made by the inmates during therapy sessions were put on sale, and artisans manned the stalls themselves. Herculia The Iron Maiden, who was actually a man, offered palm readings. Organama the one-eyed cross-eyed tattooist, offered to leave his mark on anyone game enough to let him. He was also a woman. Yeahwellah – you remember Yeahwellah – well, he and a disciple offered to sell indulgences to anyone worried about what might happen in the afterlife. Their souls could be delivered from the fires of purgatory for a price. That was my idea.

There was a children's jumping castle that proved to be a bit of a disaster. Ahmed, the resident hyperactive dragonfly, was firing on all cylinders on a full tank of fuel, and putting the entire staff on high alert for the day. From the moment the castle was inflated, he leaped all over it, climbed the towers, and crashed to the ground several times. The harder he fell, the more he wanted. Pain and adrenaline are different words but they had the same effect on the brain. Words and reprimands were wasted on him. He kept darting back and forth, bowling over everyone in his path until he was forcibly removed. Within five minutes he was back, slashing and puncturing the castle with a kitchen knife as he mumbled obscenities at the castle. It was as if a sinkhole had suddenly appeared beneath the jumping castle. The walls caved in on the children jumping, swallowing them up in the rubber beneath their feet. The public on the perimeter panicked and turned to run, leaving children and the aged to be trampled underfoot. I'm sure you've got the picture of what the incident was like.

I decided to run a stall called the Get Rich Quick. The idea was that you sold a book of 100 tickets at $1 per ticket, and you gave cash prizes amounting to $60 for certain numbers. This yielded a profit of $40 per book. At first, we were begging people to buy tickets. We said things like 'please support this worthy cause' kind of crap talk. The miserable mongrels had quickly done the sums, and as soon as the $10 lucky number went, nobody wanted to buy any more tickets.

These guys needed a bit of revving up with some *gyp stimulant* pumped into their brains, so I let it rip:

'Come on folks, get ripped off at the Get Rich Quick!' I repeatedly yelled at the top of my voice. You could visibly see the tide of people slowly turning towards our stall. People simply could not resist the temptation of beating the odds against being ripped off. It was like gambling in a casino. In the end, you're going to lose, but you refuse to believe it. Even when you do lose, you go back for more. Now that's crazy.

The tickets were selling fast and the $10, $5 and $2 prizes had all gone. The best they could get was their money back, so that's exactly what I told them. I kid you not. I called out:

'The $10, $5 and $2 prizes have all gone but you can still get ripped off at the Get Rich Quick. Get your money back at the Get Rich Quick. Roll up, roll up, ladies and gentlemen, get ripped off at the Get Rich Quick!' The more I yelled, the more they ploughed their winnings into the game. Even when it started to rain, they just kept buying tickets. Go figure. We sold 120 books that day and made $4800 profit. I had never seen so many happy faces. Being gypped works. Suckers!

Policies from the people for the people will ensure that the benefits are for the needy, not the greedy. All too often with the major parties, it's the other way around. For every intravenous dollar they give to the needy, they siphon off a small fortune for themselves by evading tax, laundering profits and plundering the government coffers with fringe benefits like helicopter flights to children's birthday parties and friends' weddings and lifetime first-class travel and pensions.

The AAA Party will introduce a whole new paradigm to the word 'government'. Based on *Aleph's World of Absurd Political Thought*, government will be restructured so that what was once the norm will become absurd and what was once considered absurd will become the norm.

Every plank in our political platform will centre on the needs of the voter and redress the present imbalance in the distribution of wealth in Umbugumbuland. Voters can choose to be categorised according to their mental predisposition rather than judged, stereotyped or demonised by a mainstream mindset that dictates what is best for them and how they should be treated.

For example, when you have a person who feels they shouldn't have to pay taxes, obey the law, stay married, pay their debts, honour their father and their mother, or anything that mainstream society today would consider an out-of-your-mind mindset, it shouldn't have to set alarm bells ringing. A progressive government in an intelligent civilised society should be able to accommodate such a mindset and categorise it so that the behaviour can be channelled into something that is productive and contributes positively to society.

A triple A Party government will issue a COIN Certificate (Certificate of Insanity) to people with this mindset. You need to be aware that once you have been issued with a COIN Certificate, you are no longer considered to be of sane mind and therefore incapable of making a will. Therefore, if you die, your affairs are put into administration and the proceeds of your estate go to the government. That's the gyp but it beats being an outcast all your life or in jail for not paying your taxes or disobeying the law or not paying your debts. It beats having to stay married if you can't stand your partner, or honouring your father and your mother if they keep treating you as a child.

This is how it works. You don't pay taxes but the money you save by not paying taxes will eventually form part of your estate and go back to the government when you die. If you don't want to obey the law, you present your COIN Certificate in a court of law and you will be assigned a place in an institution which will allow you to live out your life with people of the same mindset without being harassed by society. If you don't want to stay married, you show your partner your COIN Certificate, your partner photocopies it, and you go your own way. Your partner can then claim a support pension by attaching the photocopy to an application for a COIN partner support pension on a Form 24U. There are no questions asked and the pension is not means-tested. As a child of a COIN Certificate holder, you can apply for lifetime support on genetic inheritance grounds upon provision of a DNA certificate. Same end-of-life conditions apply.

If you don't want to pay your debts, you present your COIN Certificate and your debt is cleared. In future, you will only be able to pay for goods using cash or through a chip inserted under your skin known as an RFID (radio frequency identity) chip. The debtor can redeem the debt from the government when you die. That's a bit of a gyp because it could end up being a long wait, but the debtor can use the debt figure as a corresponding credit for collateral on an interest free government loan up to the amount that is owed.

As you can see from the examples given, there is a solution to every possible mindset problem an individual can dream up through this medium of issuing a COIN Certificate. However, you must pay a fee for that service, which in some instances can turn out to be greater than the original debt. That's the gyp.

The Department of Finance in conjunction with the Treasury will be the departments responsible for issuing the COIN certificates. There will be quite a substantial fee for a certificate because of the benefits it affords and because it lasts for a lifetime. The fee is deducted from your pension over whatever period that it takes, including the term of your natural life. That's a bit of a gyp but it's fair enough based on the principle of user pays.

These pensions are all funded by companies that pay taxes. A company is not a person, so it cannot apply for a COIN Certificate and therefore must pay taxes. That's a gyp. Any individual who is not a COIN Certificate holder must work as there is no support or safety net like unemployment benefits. They also pay taxes, which help fund the pensions. Again, if they don't want to pay taxes, they can always apply for a COIN Certificate. It shows that the AAA Party believes in equal opportunities for all.

COIN Certificate holders still must work, which is a bit of a gyp. They are public servants but pay no taxes. They are given work according to their individual limitations. Whether their work entails pressing out number plates in an institution or processing illegal immigrant forms, the pension amount is the same for all workers. In fact, you can't be a public servant unless you have a COIN Certificate. It's a perquisite. It gives you job security.

Public servants administer government policy, which is often no policy at all until the people decide they want one. They also collect the taxes from companies and self-employed people and deduct their pension from the taxes they collect, with the rest going to the government. It is in effect a services tax for the service they provide as public servants. If they don't collect enough taxes, their pensions are delayed until they do. It's an incentive based system. The government always gets paid before the pensions. That's the gyp.

Most COIN Certificate holders really believe you would have to be mad to work hard like a tradie, farmer, or in industry or as a businessman, when you can work for the government as a COIN Certificate holder and bludge most of the time. Consequently, they have no sympathy for taxpayers because they have an out and they don't want it.

For those without COIN certificates, the government also offers a NUTS (Not Utterly Sane) Certificate. This covers situations where the individuals understand they can be irrational and bordering on the insane at times because they could have accepted the COIN Certificate and been much better off. However, they did not want to carry the stigma of being perceived as insane. No system can hope to rid itself of reactionaries. NUTS certification takes less than three minutes and uses keyhole surgery that involves genetic engineering. However, it means that their offspring in 90 per cent of the cases will be born genetically lobotomised and that's the gyp.

The upside is that those offspring of NUTS certified parents are entitled to have their birth certificate endorsed so that the child becomes a dual COIN/NUTS certificate holder with all the benefits. Like fence-sitting – part COIN, part NUTS.

Because they have been genetically modified, NUTS are only suited to service in the defence forces. They have no emotional component to their psyche and only respond to orders. However, if they are found to be unsuitable for military service, which can be the case in up to 10 per cent of NUTS, they can opt for COIN certification simply by showing their ID and signing a transfer to COIN status on Form 666.

Both COIN and NUTS certificates are recyclable and can be bought from the government when the certificate holder dies. The money goes into the deceased's estate which goes back to the government anyway. The upside is that there is no way such currency can be laundered or counterfeited. So, there you have it; an ultimate 'safe' currency.

When the AAA Party is elected to government, the parliament will legislate to have the COIN and NUTS certificates legitimised as a virtual currency. The gyp for other countries is that they will never be able to manipulate our currency as it always reverts to the government as soon as its legitimate owner dies, whether that owner is in Umbugumbuland or overseas. The government will issue a set number of COIN certificates equal to the total population of Umbugumbuland at the time of the first census after the election. It will also issue an equal number of NUTS certificates which are convertible using Form 666. There is a hefty fee for the conversion and this goes to the government as well as the ongoing COIN Certificate fee every time it is transferred to a new owner. The COIN certificates can be traded as digital or crypto-currency, and that's what makes them attractive as a worldwide safe haven currency.

These tradable COIN certificates, by their finite number, will continue to grow in value as the population after the census grows organically and through immigration. The NUTS certificates equate to an option using Form 666 at any time to create a COIN Certificate that will rank equally with all the post-census COIN certificates. Therefore, the total number of COIN certificates is not finite until all the NUTS certificates have been converted.

Overseas individuals can buy COIN certificates for investment purposes or as a way of entering Umbugumbuland. However, that means they are entering Umbugumbuland as an insane person. In fact, it will be the only way for foreigners to emigrate to Umbugumbuland. In that way, there is no danger of Umbugumbuland being swamped or taken over by people from other countries because the certificates always revert to the government when the registered owner dies. It is then reissued at the going rate with the proceeds going into the government's coffers.

The allure for foreigners is that they see the certificates as a virtual Umbugumbuland COIN Club membership certificate where all the benefits are there for the taking and for the term of their natural life. From the government viewpoint, any concern about self-interest involving foreigners evaporates the moment they die. It's a win/win situation for all concerned.

Nationally, the motivation of greed for money, possessions, or earthly pleasures of the individual is tempered by the temporal nature of the currency. Ultimately, all the benefits go back to the government of the people for the people of Umbugumbulamd.

It can't get any fairer or more foolproof than that.

That's a plus.

CHAPTER 21

Just short of three months before the incumbent government ran out of time and had to face the people at the next election, rumours abounded that a new fledgling party was making inroads into the hearts and minds of 'the forgotten people'. The mainstream parties had sent out their spies and were sharpening their knives in preparation for the blood-letting and mutilation of the AAA Party as the sacrificial lamb of the forthcoming election. The hacked and bruised remains would be the road kill for all to see on every track, outback road, street and highway leading to the Palace of Power in the fun park in Cannabia.

We had no spies and no sharpened knives to do battle with our adversaries. We had no swag of multi-million dollar promises to buy our way in. We had no media outlets prepared to run the gauntlet with us. We had no jobs for the boys in jeopardy to motivate volunteers to work for us, no seasoned cut-throats, vested interests, analysts to guide us, or catalysts to convince the people we were there to lead them away from the abyss that was the mainstream parties' policies.

All we had was our slogan:

Vote AAA: We Offer You Nothing
We Keep Our Promises!

With that, the political sledging began. The sledging, which had taken so many political scalps in the past, could not attack anything our party had to offer because we offered nothing. Still, I was prepared for everything they wanted to hurl at us and I had all the replies.

> **Mainstream parties:** *AAA not fit to lead!*
> **AAA Party:** *Mainstream parties are too fat to lead because every time you shag your colleague's partner, they give you a biscuit. A vote for the mainstream parties is a biscuit to make them fatter. Don't let yourself be shagged by the privileged few; vote AAA – grassroots government of the forgotten people, by the forgotten people, for the forgotten people.*
> **Mainstream parties:** *AAA not qualified as a party!*
> **AAA Party:** *Because we don't accept biscuits from our colleagues' partners; that's unqualified party-pooping.*
> **Mainstream parties:** *The AAA Party is not endorsed by anyone who is anyone.*

AAA Party: *That's because anyone who is anyone doesn't take biscuits from just anyone.*

... and so the biscuit diplomacy continued:

Media: *Mr McNaught, we understand you spent time in a mental hospital.*

McNaught: *That's where I did my apprenticeship making biscuits for politicians' partners to feed to their partners' colleagues for favours.*

Media: *Mr McNaught, you are one of the richest people in Umbugumbuland. Why would you want to enter politics?*

McNaught: *I'm told that's where the biscuits are.*

Media: *Mr McNaught, what will be the first change you will make in the unlikely event of becoming the governing party of Umbugumbuland.*

McNaught: *Get rid of the biscuits and bring on the crumpets.*

Gradually, the fledgling AAA whirlwind began feeding on all the woes of the disenchanted. It grew and grew. Voters from the parched drought-ridden farmlands to the north and the abandoned mining quarries of the west joined up with the army of unemployed from the industrial city wastelands. Hoping their grievances might at last be addressed by the new party, they chanted in unison as they reached the outskirts of Cannabia.

'Aleph ... Aleph ... Aleph,' they cried, and followed with a moment's silence before replying with, 'A ... A ... A.'

'Aleph ... Aleph ... Aleph.'
'A ... A ... A.'

'Aleph … Aleph … Aleph.'
'A … A … A.'
'Aleph … Aleph … Aleph.'
'A … A … A.'

Soon, the juggernaut of voices from the groundswell of 'forgotten people' began to echo throughout the land. The whirly wind became a twister that sucked up supporters as it passed through every hamlet, town and city. In Cannabia, the mainstream politicians awoke in fright to the tornado that was blotting out the sun that they thought shone out of their political arses. The voters had found their voice. It was a death-defying piercing shriek.

'We'll all be ruined!' cried the politicians.

'We'll all be ruined!' was their partners' refrain.

'We'll all be ruined!' cried the media as crumpet factories began springing up all over the place and biscuit factories went broke.

But despite all the hoo-ha, nobody really believed AAA had any chance of winning the election. Yes, there was a shift, but 'No way, AAA!' was the obstinate response to the shriek. The mainstream party politicians and their partners concluded it was all just a piddle in the pond as they nibbled on the last few rations of biscuits that their colleagues had given them.

CHAPTER 22

Meanwhile, The Alliance of the Achilles Heel got wind of the threat to the status quo in Umbugumbuland that the AAA Party posed, and started burping and farting about cancelling Umbugumbuland's provisional membership of The Alliance if our party were to win government in its own right. I retorted, stating categorically that as our greatest shortcomings were embodied in the policies of the mainstream parties, then their removal from office would entitle us to claim honour credits as a preferred country without any shortcomings, as the AAA Party had no policies. Furthermore, we would build a trade wall based on such entitlements, and member countries of The Alliance would have to shoulder the costs. That would force Alliance members to pay a 15% premium on all imports from Umbugumbuland and offer a 15% discount on all exports to Umbugumbuland. As well, the honour credits gave Umbugumbuland pre-emptive rights over all commodities, goods and services that The Alliance member countries offered. This was in their constitution.

The elbow jerk reaction of Woccowaccaland, Central Lilulaland and Allalalaland was to deny our claim to honour credits, but as soon as Woccowaccaland realised that it meant they would be agreeing with Allalalaland (whose religious views were opposite), they withdrew their objection. Allalalaland in turn withdrew its objection so that it would not appear to be allied in any way with Central Lilulaland, which had no religion. Central Lilulaland decided to withdraw its objection as soon as North Lilulaland offered to annex Umbugumbuland and build military bases with nuclear warhead capacity that were in range of every major city in Central Lilulaland. This made Ellifafaland so angry that they put in a counter offer to Umbugumbuland to build military bases with nuclear warhead capacity and launch communication satellites, giving Umbugumbuland unparalleled internet access to the remotest corner of the land. Suwajiland decided that its national security would be compromised if Ellifafaland launched extra communication satellites. They made an offer to annex Umbugumbuland, build military bases with nuclear warhead capacity, and launch communication satellites giving Umbugumbuland unparalleled internet access as well as providing every house with a digital TV. Not to be outdone, Woccowaccaland further offered to annex Umbugumbuland, build military bases with nuclear warhead capacity and launch communication satellites which would give Umbugumbuland unparalleled internet access as well as provide every house with a digital TV and a plasticised, elasticised table.

That's where the bidding stopped, probably because none of the member countries had ever heard of a plasticised, elasticised table and could not put a value on it. I made it known to all of them that if the AAA Party won government, it would not be interested in trading its integrity in return for the trivial playthings they were offering. Nevertheless, many mainstream party members immediately made secret offers to switch allegiance to the AAA Party if we did not win the election in our own right and if we were prepared to accept the highest offer from any other country.

The AAA Party was now in a sweet spot. The media moguls, who were originally on the side of the mainstream parties, decided to switch allegiance and give our party some very favourable press. They didn't want to be left out; favourable press coverage was all they had to offer in the hope that in the event of a triple A victory, they would be able to claim some of the kudos.

Scupper, Blithe, Thee and I had 'cabinet meetings' in the dark to decide on a whole range of issues arising from our change of fortune and the prospect of winning the 'unwinnable election'. The idea was that I would make a proposal and each of us who agreed would raise their hand. I would then turn on the light to be amazed that every decision was unanimous. Go figure. No wonder we were on a winner; we were all of one mind. We were invincible, but the game was far from over.

In the lead up to the election, The Alliance member countries began bank-rolling the four major mainstream parties to keep us out of government and thereby avoid forking out the honour credits that

Umbugumbuland would be entitled to if the AAA Party won government. The mainstream parties changed tack and put all their energy into a last-ditch attempt to besmirch my character and cast doubts on my capacity to rule. They demanded access to my medical files, insisting that if I was not of sane mind, then I would be compelled to exit the race for president of Umbugumbuland. I refused and threatened to sue any doctors, psychologists, psychiatrists, medical staff or hospitals for breach of patient confidentiality if they so much as whispered any information that might be on any of my files. With that avenue blocked, they then managed to dig up information on my birth father that even I had not known. The sad fact was that I was conceived in a one night stand after a Hoopla University orientation week function where my mother and birth father met for the first and last time.

It turns out my birth father was the son of a farmer who also raised a few sheep. He cultivated some summer wheat crops on an incredibly inhospitable outcrop of stony country in the highlands overlooking the sea east of Hoopla City. He built a crofter's hut from stone, grass, bark and mud, and because he was quite eccentric, his wife (my grandmother) left him, and he lived in that hut with his son, my father. As soon as the master tacticians from the mainstream parties unearthed the scent of eccentricity in my family history, they began researching my father's history, hoping to discover the mother lode in their search for 'crazy' genes.

That's when I discovered where I got my brains. My father was identified as a Mensa early in his primary school years. He was offered a provincial scholarship to continue his studies at high school where he matriculated as dux of the prestigious Lingalonga Lovelorn Academy for Gifted Students. He went on to Hoopla University on a full scholarship that paid for accommodation, a small living wage and full tuition fees. He stayed at Hoopla for twenty-five years and gained degrees in maths, science and the arts before specialising in studies in philosophy. In philosophy, he progressed through the ranks from tutor, associate lecturer, research associate to lecturer, research fellow to senior lecturer, senior research fellow to associate professor, reader to professor. So, while my stepfather, Jack, was giving me a beating, my dad was sitting pretty at the top of the dung pile at Hoopla University.

That all changed one morning when he was informed that his father had passed away. His colleagues and his friends were shocked and dismayed when he resigned and left the university for good. He insisted he was obliged to take over the family farm. It was, I stress, a very ordinary farm. Apart from the magnificent ocean view, it offered scant returns despite the extraordinary efforts needed to get those returns. His friends and colleagues, fearing the strange turnaround in his life's journey was a result of some sort of mental breakdown from the shock loss of his father, implored him to take stock of his situation and consider returning to the university. He refused. When they reminded him of the work he had put into his education, the amount of State money spent on his education, and the faith they placed in him for an illustrious career and what a waste it would all be, he responded with one sentence: 'My education is never lost'. Go figure.

The more I think about it, the more I figure he'd have to be mad to go back to his father's stony patch of good-for-nothing earth. In fact, such a deed would certainly qualify for a COIN Certificate in my new administration when it comes to pass that AAA wins government.

Thus, any glister of hope the mainstream parties had that I might have some 'crazy' genes faded. Their malice only strengthened my resolve. It materialised as a great positive for my ego – that I was bright as or maybe even brighter than I thought I was.

A few weeks before the election, other idiosyncrasies began to emerge from within the fabric of our 'silent' society. There were those who were envious of my wealth. There were those who were resentful of my status; after all, I was the grandson of an eccentric crofter and son of a self-exiled academic. There were those who were covetous of my lifestyle, begrudging of my intellect, and spiteful towards me because of the threat I posed to their layabout careers bludging on the people of Umbugumbuland.

Well, it was going to be show time with a bang for all those guys.

CHAPTER 23

For the last week of the campaign, every AAA Party candidate in every electorate was directed to find a venue where they could light a 'campfire' (which was really a bonfire) and invite everyone to sit with them by the fire to chat and to partake of the AAA Party bully beef stew. We offered the people the opportunity to make suggestions for what they considered to be good government. These suggestions could be written down and placed in a suggestion box beside the campfire. Beside it was a donation box for those who felt they really wanted to be a part of making it all happen by donating a gold coin as a gesture of support for the party.

Above and behind each dazzling campfire was a huge, red, lorry-sized banner. It read:

AAA Party Campfire Campaign

TRUST US … We Offer You Nothing … TRUST US
– We Keep Our Promises –
– We can help get you what you want –

- **Make some suggestions**
- **Try our bully beef stew**
- **Make a gold coin donation**

The campaign was set to continue for seven days and seven nights before election day. The *modus operandi* of this part of the campaign was so ridiculous that soon everybody turned up just to check it out. Some people came for the fire; the homeless came for the bully beef stew, and many people gave a gold coin donation. The donation was their way of saying 'stick it up yours' to the mainstream parties.

The TV cameras whirred as the journalists went wild interviewing the candidates and the voters in the street. The old, aged, infirm in wheelchairs, and even children, backpackers, and tourists revelled in the excitement generated. Spontaneous campfire love-fests, inspired by music and dance, exploded out of little pockets of what was originally just a gathering of inquisitive people. Like a wildfire, the number of campfires grew and grew across the nation until people began building their own in their own backyards, asking for suggestions, offering bully beef stew and calling for gold coin donations for the party.

The pattern was the same everywhere. On the first night, people came to wonder. On the second night, they came to see what the fuss was all about from others telling them. By the third night, people brought their own drinks and began singing and dancing to the music. The fourth night marked what turned out to be the beginning of a three-day festival. Everyone wanted to party.

The local councils provided portable dunnies and running water. Police were trucked in to Cannabia and the capital cities from nearby villages and outstations to maintain law and order. Ambulances and community services officers were stationed on site to deal with injuries, hyperventilation, lost children and drug-related emergencies. The AAA Campfire Campaign had snowballed and it was rocking!

On the last night, many venues had to relocate to cow paddocks and footy ovals to cope with the crowds, and on election day, everyone turned up at the ballot boxes to vote. The people wanted to have their voice heard.

Within a few hours of the polls closing across the country, it became clear that the AAA Party had won in a landslide. The people had finally participated in the process of determining their own destinies and had given the AAA Party a resounding mandate to govern in its own right.

To celebrate, everyone locked arms and marched down the streets uttering a catchcry that began sweeping the country:

'Up your nose with a rubber hose. Cut the crap, it's a wipe-out!'

The hands went up after each cry, and with the middle fingers extended towards the sky they cried, 'Yeah!'

They were in control for the first time ever. They were the government of the people even though they had no clue what kind of government it would be because we offered them nothing but bully beef stew which no-one ate in the end because, frankly, it tasted like shit.

CHAPTER 24

The initial reaction from many of the member countries of The Alliance was to send emissaries immediately to Umbugumbuland. They wanted to meet with me to try to make the best of what they perceived to be a bad situation. For example, many of the trade deals and special concessions that had been negotiated with the previous government were now in limbo, and the palms they had greased along the way were no longer of any use to them.

There was an exodus of foreign diplomats fearing charges of corruption, involvement in scams and other types of conduct unbecoming. Many secret services personnel followed suit for many of the same reasons, as well as spying with intent to bring down a nation. So already, the country was beginning to cleanse itself of its cancers.

Ironically, many other countries began to see Umbugumbuland as a land of opportunity because the absence of policies meant the political vacuum was most enticing. This absence of matter (vacuum) defined our government. Outsiders wanting to invest in our country would find less pressure to conform, less red tape, fewer constraints through complex laws, less interference by bureaucrats, and less scrutiny of company affairs. All of this led to greater autonomy and independence.

Umbugumbuland soon became the toast of the international investment community. Countries with tight capital controls were prepared to allow money to flow out of their countries into this new anything-goes economy because it meant gaining a guaranteed foothold in a free and open economy. Enterprises in powerful, tightly controlled economies needed to expand overseas to escape the rigid constraints of their own economies to continue to grow.

Soon a huge flotilla of money carriers from all the wealthy Alliance countries had their GPSes set for Umbugumbuland. They daily ploughed through tempestuous seas towards our borders, with the flimsy craft of the poorer nations following in their wake. The Umbugumbuan COIN, as a crypto-currency, was about to become the holy grail of world currencies, and he who controlled the COIN, controlled The Alliance.

Yes!

CHAPTER 25

Number 666 isn't just the number of the form used to convert a NUTS Certificate to a COIN Certificate. In mathematics, 666 is the sum of the first 36 'natural numbers'. That is 1 + 2 + 3 + 4 ... + 34 + 35 + 36 = 666. That makes it what is called a 'triangular number'. The numbers 15 and 21 are also triangular numbers, and together 15 + 21 = 36, and if you add the square of 15 to the square of 21 you get 666. Also, 666 is the sum of the squares of the first seven prime numbers 2, 3, 5, 7, 11, 13, and 17.

Before you get too involved in the mathematics of the number, it is sufficient to know that 666 is a special number in more ways than one. The Roman numeral for 666, DCLXVI has exactly one occurrence of all symbols whose value is less than 1000: D = 500, C = 100, L = 50, X = 10, V = 5, I = 1. Almost spooky really.

So, without going into explicit formulas involving binomial coefficients, 666 is part of a phenomenon that I can explain using a simple experiment. You place 36 square wooden blocks in a row on a table and on top of those you place 35 blocks followed by 34 blocks, then 33 blocks, right down to the final one block at the top. The phenomenon is that it forms an equilateral triangle with a total of 666 blocks.

Why am I telling you all this? Because it will help you to understand how I think, and you must remember what I told you way back when my stepfather was beating me up how they worked it out that I was off the charts as far as intelligence measures go. You see, when I talked about offering the people of Umbugumbuland 'nothing' in return for their vote, it wasn't because I was a 'crazy', it was because I was smart; well-above-average smart, probably more like Mensa-smart. By applying the principle of physics to the affairs and ways of people, catching their votes was as certain as fresh apple in a possum trap.

What I called 'vacuum (absence of matter) rule' was inspired by applying the characteristics of a vacuum to the needs of the people. I wanted them to see AAA as the party they could trust; that offered them nothing, but at least didn't lie about it. The party was upfront about the fact that politics was just a gyp. The moment it occurred to the everyday punters that they were continually being gypped, they were sucked into our way of thinking that we could be a government of the forgotten people, by the forgotten people, for the forgotten people.

So, what's that got to do with the mathematics of the number 666? As I said, it's to help you understand how I think. I figured if we could envisage Umbugumbuland as an equilateral triangle (all sides being equal) then we need to ensure that everything in the governing of that country is logical, interconnected, accounted for, makes sense and is as close to the perfect science in the mathematical phenomenon of the number 666 (which you now understand because I explained it to you). It's more about enlightenment. Things don't have to be the way they always were; they can be a lot closer to what we want them to be. All the mainstream parties had the tail of the dolphin the wrong way around, just like Pencil Fingers, his mate and the smartarse shrink Dr Freudfellow at the Hoopla Hospital Mental 'Ward War 1' back in the day. They were so used to the picture of the dolphin in the coffee shop with the tail the wrong way around that it became the norm for them. That denied the lie. People were living the lie because someone had presented it as the truth. It's a bit like false memories or even what fake news could end up doing to society.

By the end of the first 100 days in government, all the groundwork for good government had been completed, and good government was beginning to happen. The future of the country was now entrenched in the care of Aleph's Army for Armageddon. The people had nothing to worry about. They had nothing to fear and could be happy. All that remained to be done was for the government to wait for the population of Umbugumbuland to be determined at the next census. It could then legislate the issue of COIN certificates as a crypto-currency to provide many tangible benefits to the people and the country. Our system, despite its dual currency, would be the envy of all The Alliance countries.

My concern at that point was where to from here and with whom? The party, in the short term at least, had dealt with the dangers from without, namely the opposition parties and foreigners meddling in our country's affairs. There would have to be demons who had their own agenda and self-interest at heart that had to be rooted out within our own party. Such group activities, often covert and clandestine yet very destabilising, were not always clearly visible or predictable.

It was time for me to take myself out of the Palace of Power and separate myself completely from that vantage point. Of course, Blithe and Scupper would have to come with me because I needed to run all my thoughts past them to ensure I was considering all problems and solutions from other perspectives.

That left Thee in charge of the government. That's you the reader, remember? You're one of the forgotten people who must start taking responsibility for their own government. This is probably where even you, Thee, might be prepared to accept that I could be crazy, so I'm going to give you the benefit of the doubt. I'm going to have myself committed to a mental health facility in Woccowaccaland to determine once and for all whether I'm crazy or just ahead of my time.

I intend to enter the country incognito under a false passport and in the company and care of my personal psychologist Blithe. My guise as a mental patient meant everyone would have to respect my confidentiality and nobody would be able to find any trace of me until I decided to resurface in Umbugumbuland. Scupper would administer all my business interests from abroad. It would then be all up to Thee to keep the cannons firing here at home. So, in answer to my previous question of 'Where to from here and with whom?', the answer is Woccowaccaland with Scupper and Blithe.

I chose a place abroad because I really wanted to view the situation in Umbugumbuland through the eyes, ears, nose and throat of those political savages of The Alliance. From there I would understand what was influencing their thinking and be able to pre-empt their every move and take the necessary decisive action to counter any impact it might have on Umbugumbuland.

Within days, my disappearance became front page news in Woccowaccaland. The president had vanished without a trace. Maybe he was kidnapped and the kidnappers had commanded the government to deny it. Maybe he was dead and the kidnappers were hiding the fact. Everything that could possibly go wrong did go wrong, according to all the media analysts and conspiracy theorists. Little did they know that I was safe and snug in my little white gown pretending to swallow my rainbow-coloured assortment of pills as I read the crap that people all over the world couldn't wait to be told.

What was most interesting to read and hear, smell and digest was the astonishment with which the pundits overseas assessed the impact of a missing president on the state of affairs in Umbugumbuland. They gargled words of wonder as their teeth rattled on about a country seemingly in complete control, without the slightest hint of chaos on the streets or in the market place. Finally, they figured our public servants (who you and I know were certified insane) were so adept at running the country that there was obviously no need for a leader in our perfect political state, and that perhaps

The Alliance countries should consider getting rid of their own heads of state.

They would not let the matter rest. Eventually, one academic from Woccowaccaland got wind of the COIN certificates that had to be issued before public servants could qualify for the job. This academic claimed that because she was a woman, she could assess the matter with a maternal calm that all men lacked. She said the answer was quite simple although she refused to tell anyone what it was. She insisted she did not want to deprive anyone of the thrill of the discovery when it finally came to them. Another academic from Ellifafaland claimed the matter needed to be assessed at a metaphysical level of thinking, which was why the public could never grasp such a concept. He did not elucidate on this because it would be beyond anyone's comprehension anyway. A third pundit and self-confessed cannibal from East Blahblahland claimed that it proved that cannibals acquired the power of their victims as he had devoured an Umbugumbuan backpacker and subsequently predicted their president would disappear.

This latest statement sparked fears that maybe I was the Umbugumbuan who the cannibal had devoured, and he was summarily executed at the hands of his own people. He was 'necklaced' with a burning rubber tyre filled with petrol. No more statements came out of East Blahblahland after that.

In Allalalaland, the high priests insisted that the people of Umbugumbuland had shown through their exemplary behaviour that they were ready to give up sex. This placed them within easy reach of the 'Holiest State'. In battle-torn East Lilulaland, people began to sing the praises of a country obviously at peace with itself, and agreed to a ceasefire for thirty-six hours. This would allow opposing forces to return the severed arms and legs of their enemies, and the decapitated heads that had been kept as trophies.

No country wanted to be left out of showing how the conduct of Umbugumbuans provided a role model for all. In West Blahblahland, drug lords from the Organisation of Drug Exporting Countries (ODEC) agreed to set aside a percentage of all their profits to hire people from Umbugumbuland with COIN certificates to train their public servants in the hope that it might help address the rampant drug-related violence in their countries. This statement immediately created a huge spike in demand for COIN certificates and their value in Umbugumbuland. I could see that by the way we were going, COIN certificates would eventually rival superannuation as a retirement nest-egg.

In South Lilulaland, the banana republic with a monkey-see-monkey-do mentality, the president and vice-president were assassinated within a week of each other in the hope that the country's problems would disappear and everyone would become rich. In Central Lilulaland, they finally came up with an original thought to ban the media, the internet and cease all contact of its citizens with the outside world. North Lilulaland eagerly followed suit as their president was re-elected in a landslide on the promise that COIN certificates would soon be available there.

Thus it went on and on and soon my absurd manifesto entitled Aleph's World of Absurd Political Theory was coined as 'Absurdism'. Had I not returned to Umbugumbuland, I have no doubt I would have been revered as its founding father and secured my place in the history of political ideologies.

I could never have imagined that my new political system would be perceived as such a success by all those other countries, and that my reinvention of myself as a politician was the phoenix rising yet again from the ashes of the ashes of the good-for-nothing, dead-loss-to-society that everyone wanted to believe I was.

CHAPTER 26

I felt a certain pride when I stood up in The Yodelling Chamber in The Palace of Power (the name Clipjoint had been removed) to deliver my first address to the people since my reappearance in Umbugumbuland. The public gallery was overflowing with reporters, mums and dads, school children with their teachers, and a significant presence of foreigners. Outside, several bands were belting out a feast of sounds in reggae, folk, hip hop, jazz, pop, country, metal and punk. Soon, the old campaign chorus rose above it all:

'Aleph … Aleph … Aleph.' A moment's silence and then the reply, 'A … A… A.'

'Aleph … Aleph … Aleph.'
'A … A … A.'
'Aleph … Aleph … Aleph.'
'A … A … A.'
'Aleph … Aleph … Aleph.'
'A … A … A.'

As all eyes turned towards me, I commenced my address to the people of Umbugumbuland.

'My beloved fellow Umbugumbuans, not too long ago we were a nation at war; with ourselves. Yet today we stand united against the world. United as in equal … United as in free … United as in purpose … to make Umbugumbuland greater than it has ever been before. We are the envy of every member country of The Alliance.

'Now we are put to the test. Against what odds can we survive? Every last brick that is our resolve, that our fortress of freedom should stand, is a brick laid by the forgotten people of this great country. If you are one of those forgotten people, rise up your heart and take a bow. If you are one who plots against us, hang your head in shame.

'For forty days and forty nights I was becalmed in a political wilderness in my search for the directions that would ensure we remain free, and you have delivered them to me. Here in this Palace of Power with its leader in absentia, you did not falter, you did not fail, you did not yield, and the rest of the world salutes you. I did not return to a country in chaos worshipping a golden calf as Moses did and other countries do. I returned to the calm of a cool and collected people in complete control. You stood by the time-honoured principle, preserved in the blood of war, that when the flag-bearer falls, the next person picks up the flag and so on to the very last soldier. We shall never surrender our cause!

'We owe it to those who went before us to keep this country great and acknowledge that their work and their sacrifices were not in vain. You have shown that we

can keep it great; free from fear of chaos and oppression, free from meddlers and manipulators, and free from the corrupt and the selfish.

'This Palace of Power has been delivered as a safe house by our Army for Armageddon. It is the location for the gathering of the clans that once were parties in opposition to one another and now are one. United we stand against the forces of evil, against the world, and against all odds — forever free under the government of the forgotten people, by the forgotten people, for the forgotten people.

'Thank you all.'

A tumultuous roar echoed through the chamber, the alcoves and the corridors of power as Aleph's Military Marching Band marched the crowds to the bottom of the hill and then marched them back again. Every radio, television, iPhone and iPad was tuned into Aleph's Address to the Nation.

Inside the safe house, as a final gesture to all on the fickleness of human nature, I reached into a huge bag of lollies and chocolates and threw handful after handful towards the opposition party members. Despite their swollen feet from lack of exercise, their fattened faces from over-indulging on biscuits, and red from being out of breath, all found the energy to spring to their feet and trample one another like turkeys vying for the corn. Good old tramplers, inspired partly out of self-interest and partly out of the desire to self-harm. Suckers!

CHAPTER 27

After my historic speech, I began examining ways of determining strategies for the smooth transition away from a system of government that was from the top down with a head of state or its equivalent, to one that would be run by the forgotten people – the COINs – from the bottom up.

I decided the best way to effect the transition would be to utilise technology to enable leadership in government to go on auto-pilot and run itself. If auto-pilot could enable a plane to fly and land, and self-drive cars to drive themselves and park, surely a government on auto-pilot without a head of state should be able to function with just public servants and prosper.

The difficulty would be finding enough COINs to ensure the smooth running of government at different points of time in the future, because abstract determinants such as those defining 'state of mind' can be difficult to identify by qualifications and interview alone. Determinants of 'state of mind' need to be identifiable much earlier and with more certainty. This could only be done at the cellular level of the *ribosome* which is the interface between genetic information and how things actually appear.

Therefore, to bypass the tedious and often misleading process of interviewing persons with set qualifications, the determiners of 'state of mind' could be isolated through genetic sampling in the amniocentesis prenatal test. That test is carried out between the 15th and 18th week of pregnancy and is 99.4% accurate. It doesn't get much better than that.

Many mothers, as part of the condition of pregnancy, are required by their doctors to take the test to determine birth defects and to provide other important genetic related information. A small amount of amniotic fluid is extracted and sent to the laboratory.

The analysis of the sample is then extended to look for precursors to insanity. If the test comes back positive for insanity at the genetic level, then the child will be issued with a COIN Certificate at birth and the result would remain confidential until the child attains the age of 16 years. Any time after that, the individual can fill out a Form 666 (a) – Request to Access Results of Amniocentesis. If the individual discovers he or she has been issued with a COIN Certificate at birth, then all the benefits become an entitlement to be enjoyed for life including a career in the public service. If the individual chooses to keep it a secret, then the certificate would remain in safe-keeping until a claim is made. On death, the right to claim it expires and reverts to the government.

Intensive educational programs would be put in place over three years to encourage mothers to take the test which would be free. The data on all newborn babies would be recorded on a national database. For those mothers who do not wish to conform, there would be levies imposed against their earnings for the next sixteen years. This would go into a fund to support children with birth defects. The levy would amount to a substantial sum over that period, and mothers would have to be mad not to agree to take the prenatal test.

CHAPTER 28

Once the government was locked in to auto-pilot, I found I had made so much money from my real estate development ventures, stock exchange trading, casinos, golf courses and hotels and restaurants that I became bored with the idea of making money. With Scupper in charge of managing my investments, I could distance myself from thoughts of making more money, although it happened anyhow as the momentum of many of the enterprises continued and the businesses grew by inertia.

Blithe was content with the side benefits of being First Lady. The position brought her into the company of many of the great thinkers at home and from abroad. She got to meet with them by default when they were unable to get an audience with me. She openly encouraged them to speak their minds and share their views. They were mostly people who at some stage of their lives became disenchanted with the ways of the world, and in that sense, were travelling life journeys parallel to mine. Who better to speak to about that than Blithe?

Mostly their thoughts came back to laments for the human condition. They all had answers. Only the guise for delivering them was different. It was basically one or a combination of religion, philosophy, history, art, literature, anthropology, psychology or biology.

I abandoned religion when I lost Yeahwellah. Pragmatism was the shear pin that disengaged philosophy as a political solution. History, art and literature were always running into dead ends, providing no formulaic solutions whatsoever. They were only playthings; tools for 'greater mortals' to frustrate and confuse 'lesser mortals'. Only anthropology offered some semblance of order and explanation of the condition as a cultural phenomenon. Psychology was too chaotic and biology too simplistic.

The more I thought about and talked about the human condition with Blithe, the more I felt myself becoming the black sheep drowning again. The downward spiral that was an everlasting black hole drained me of my energies and crippled my willpower to keep on keeping on. I who had everything to live for, suddenly only wanted to lay it all to rest with one last guttural gasp. I could see the curtain falling, calling me to go backstage.

That KO'd me, but I got up again. My brain was overheating. I went into overdrive hoping the drag on all the cogs would slow me down and lessen the blow of the next KO that was about to come. I could smell the brake linings burning and I came to a halt with a blunt thud. My cheekbones were sucked in and with nostrils flared, goggle-eyed and in a state of '*zuck*' where life sucks, I was out for the count.

I was a mess, but when I recovered, I collected all the broken glass and glued myself back together again. A glimmer of hope reflected as I told myself I would not accept this as the end. It cheered me up and all the cracks filled over and I was whole again. I sensed the déjà vu and then there was a quickening. Maybe 'feeling whole again' would not last as long this time. I feared I might not be able to achieve as much in this half-life and that maybe the quickening would be cruel this time.

I gathered my thoughts, took some pills, smoked some pot and found myself floating on an orange-coloured rubber dingy in a nowhere sea with my thoughts all crisp and icicled over. The images were all of me as a forgotten person among all the other forgotten people, then the curtain lifted and interval was over and the next Act had already kicked off.

You have no idea what a relief it was to realise there was still another half-life to go. I vowed to get it right this time, which meant I had to get my head right first. I had to get my affairs in order.

I was able to 'vacate' my position as president of Umbugumbuland and still get paid (not because I needed the money but because I wanted to be assured that I was still the president) without anybody realising. This was because the system was set up and flourishing as a bottom-up '*lowerarchial*' system of government. Of course, I could always make myself available in the unlikely event that I might be needed to serve tea or carry drinks, which made me feel quite at ease about it all.

Those thoughts and images brought me to the realisation that I was ready to get help for my own state of mind. I had myself voluntarily committed to the psychiatric hospital in Mocknot Falls in Woccowaccaland to get the help I needed to survive this second half of my life. They already had a patient file on me under my pseudonym of Wattle McBottle from the time I stayed there to assess the state and standing of Umbugumbuland under AAA Party 'vacuum rule'.

I was admitted to my old Ward 24/7. A lot of the previous inmates and staff were still there as it was not all that long ago that I was there. Those who remembered me welcomed me back with a gargle or a limp-one, step-two, step-back-step or some other out-of-the-ordinary signal of recognition. Some even remembered my nickname, Watto. It was home again klakkity-klock, and I was looking forward to my rehabilitation.

However, this time it was different because I went alone and was actually taking medication. There was a new warden in charge who had zero tolerance for any inmates who dared imagine they had a mind of their own. That really made me arc up and rise to the challenge. It was a big mistake. The other mistake was that I didn't just up and leave while I still could before I was zonked out with medication. I don't know what it was that made me believe I was still in control when really, I was far from it. Anyhow, it was now too late because I was already a marked man and the warden wasn't going to let me go anywhere. I kicked back hard, deciding to revisit my rebellious youth and be ruled by my instinct rather than be guided by my intellect.

It was I who was outclassed this time. I was outwitted by the passage of time and the new methodology and procedures for dealing with mischievous, belligerent and recalcitrant inmates. Indeed, it didn't take me long to realise that the warden at Mocknot Falls Psychiatric Hospital ran the show more like the old lunatic asylums as opposed to a respite centre. The slightest misbehaviour would result in a 'code' being called, a bashing by hospital security, or hours in a padded cell, or both. On top of that, drugs were prescribed that often caused brain seizures and anaphylaxis or horrendous weight gain. The most persuasive of all was the electroconvulsive therapy. Even Wattle McBottle, aka Aleph McNaught, the president of Umbugumbuland, was not immune to the psychological terror that was electroconvulsive therapy.

There were only some very short intervals between medication and 'therapy' when I could collect my thoughts enough to try to work out how to elude the beaters that kept wanting to scramble my brains. Everything I needed or could use had been locked away, including my phone, wallet and passport. In the 69 years since it was built (which was exactly my age on this admittance), Mocknot Falls Psychiatric Hospital had never had a patient escape because it was designed to house inmates who were criminally insane. As well, I couldn't get far without my wallet much less out of the country without my passport.

My prospects were beginning to look quite bleak and I began having anxiety attacks. Padded cells and straitjackets and double doses of I know not what wore me down and convinced me it was time to start thinking laterally. I went on my best behaviour for a whole fortnight, and each day the nurses began to pay less and less attention to me.

During that time, I also spent much of my time convincing two younger short-fused inmates to mutiny against their detention. The good old steel-chair-through-the-window trick had never failed in the past and it wasn't going to fail these two guys either, I assured them.

One morning as the warden was doing his rounds, I gave them the pre-arranged signal for the most opportune moment to hurl the chairs, and the deed was done. Inmates scattered and the warden with his entourage compared jaw-drops as they looked at each other and froze. I took a flying leap towards the smaller of the two, knocking him to the ground and restraining him in a headlock. His accomplice took to me with two long shards of glass and began ripping into both my arms and screaming at me to let go of his mate.

Security eventually came to my rescue and I was rushed off to First Aid before being drugged with pain killers and thrown into a padded cell. What? That was nowhere in the script. That was not supposed to happen.

When I began responding to the bright lights, the rib jabs and the face slaps an hour, three hours, a day or three days later, I guessed I was in deep shit. So much for my act of heroism! In Umbugumbuland I would have been given the keys to the city and a fistful of cash as reward money. Here, two burly wardsmen lifted me like a wet rag with my arms all bandaged up and my toes just touching the ground and bundled me into the warden's office. Surprisingly, it was not the stern-faced lock-jawed killer commando that faced me now but his alter ego – a pussy-whipped nerd of a worm of the lowest order with only one orifice which he ate with, shat from and spoke out of. Of course, I would never tell him that, and I even thought about it really quietly so that it was impossible for him to imagine what I was thinking. No, I was going to be especially diplomatic at least for just this once.

The orifice spoke. It commended me for my bravery in tackling the first chair-chucker and apologised to me for having suffered the stab wounds to my arms from his accomplice. It then invited me to sit opposite the warden at his desk where I could see he had a file with my name on it. He remarked that the file revealed I was a foreigner and a previous inmate with an impeccable prior behaviour record.

I was pleased to hear that but I wondered what happened to the fact that I had admitted myself voluntarily. He asked me if I had been happy with my treatment to date. Fortunately, I had the presence of mind to say that I couldn't be happier and he was pleased with that. I followed it up quickly with a statement that I had a commitment to return to my various business interests in Umbugumbuland, and even quicker with a statement that I would like to show my appreciation by making a substantial donation to the Mocknot Falls Psychiatric Hospital as a gesture of appreciation for what they had done for me so that they could get on with their good work.

He asked me how I expected to be able to do that when there was no evidence that Wattle McBottle had any assets overseas and that my treatment was being funded totally by a very lucrative grant to The Alliance headquarters in Woccowaccaland from an anonymous donor in Umbugumbuland. Based on that misinformation, my brain quickly computed that there was a conspiracy going on that neither of us knew anything about and that I was in deep shit. He added that the grant was the main reason I was being kept at Mocknot Falls and he would expect that any hope I had of getting out by way of a 'gesture of appreciation' would need to be greater than that offered to The Alliance to keep me there. I assured him it was and that if he told me the figure, I would double it. Of course, he agreed without further ado.

I asked if I could have access to a computer so that I could make the transfer of money that would assure him of my good intentions. He quickly obliged but after I brought up the Umbugumbuland Development Bank website, I found I could not remember my Client Identification Number and suspected the medication had scrambled my brain for numbers. When I told him I couldn't remember my Client Identification Number, he said he wasn't surprised because the medication I was receiving had probably scrambled my brain for numbers. He added that to discharge his duty of care, he had to be sure that I was ready to be released on my own recognisance. Remembering my Client Identification Number would make it a lot easier for him to make that decision.

I was given a small comfortable room beside his office. It had a couch, desk with a computer, drinks fridge, snack bar and bars on the window. I racked my brain for two days for the elusive Client Identification Number. On the third day, when the warden's secretary informed me that my time was up and that I would be returning to my Ward 24/7 that evening, I decided that the only way was to hack the website and go in through the back-end.

When the wardsmen came that evening to return me to Ward 24/7, I could tell them that I had executed the transfer and all the money would be through in the next 24 hours. They communicated my message to the warden and I was returned immediately to my comfortable room. Within an hour a gourmet four-course meal was delivered with ice, champagne, beer, spirits and soft drinks.

Next day the warden invited me into his office, and on his desk were my mobile phone, wallet and passport. He told me that he had incurred some personal expenses to arrange for the grants to be annulled, as they were an impediment to my release and if I could return the amount to his account, he would be much obliged. He pointed to a piece of paper on which was written an account number and an amount of money.

I leaned over to look at the amount and could see that the website for the Umbugumbuland Development Bank was already up on his desktop computer. I entered my Client Identification Number and my password, navigated the task, typed in the amount and pressed 'Enter'. It was a five-figure sum, which left me wondering about the nature of his next request.

He did not disappoint me. By that I do not mean he asked me for more money. I mean he was true to his word and I was accompanied to the airport by the warden himself in a stretch limo. Within 24 hours I would be back in Umbugumbuland where I would pursue the reason The Alliance wanted me to remain in Woccowaccaland and who the mongrel was back home that had put them up to it.

I had to be careful.

I had become fragile.

CHAPTER 29

I did not return to Umbugumbuland with an uncontrollable rage or an obsession for revenge over what had happened to me. Instead, I returned with a new mindset prepared to root out an enemy that wanted me dead, or worse, to die slowly and in great pain. I had to develop a strategy where I was meticulous in everything I did and I had to remain undercover as the forever calm and in control master of the mind game.

To be a master at mind games you must know your adversary. You must be able to get in between their ears and rattle their balance until they topple and fall. My strategy of choice involved an in-depth persona analysis; a homebrand application of the principles of psychoanalysis. *Persona analysis* is my technique for exploring and understanding various mental disorders. Understand the disorder and you own the person, just like I owned Yeahwellah and Scupper.

Persona analysis does not involve person to person interaction in the way psychoanalysis does. It involves imagining what responses might be elicited from a target individual under hypnosis. The profile that emerges is the game changer that enables you to pre-empt the anticipated event and foil or neutralise any impact it might have on the overall game you are playing. The champion tennis player is a master of mind games through this aspect of his or her persona profile.

Persona profiling enabled me to whittle down the list of suspects that I had compiled on my journey back to Umbugumbuland from Woccowaccaland. Primary analysis was quickly conducted in my mind in flight. It led me to conclude the obvious that the suspect would have to be mad to take me on in the first place. By mad I mean you had to have a mind that was completely irrational and unfathomable and you had to conduct yourself in a manner that suggested a random, chaotic based operative whose every action was camouflaged by confusion as is the intent of disorientation deployed in a maze of mirrors, for example.

By the time I had landed, I knew it had to be either Scupper or Blithe or both. Only they had the innate capacity to even attempt such a challenge to my authority because as mindsets, they were a creation from within my own psyche. Could it be possible that either one or the other or both had imposed that death wish on me?

Scupper had given up gambling to deliver both a wealth that was beyond our wildest dreams. Scupper, the left hemisphere of my brain; my focus for processing information in analytical and sequential ways and then verbalising it to make things happen. He was my digital brain that controlled my writing, reading, calculation and logical thinking.

Or was it Blithe? Blithe was the other half of my brain; the right hemisphere. How could I function without her? She represented my visual take on every situation. She enabled me to process information intuitively. She was my analogue brain which gave me a three-dimensional sense and allowed me to be creative and artistic.

The answers could only be delivered through *persona analysis* and nobody knew them both as well as I did or at least thought I did.

For Blithe the hypno-persona profile offered up three possible sources. They were *penis envy*, her *super persona* and her *sotto persona*. *Penis envy* would account for the fetish Blithe had for trampling males, and I was male. I imagined that in her psychosexual development as a young girl, Blithe would have experienced anxiety upon realisation that she did not have a penis. As an adult, she would eventually realise that she could never be me. I was the ultimate male persona. That would have to be a motive. All that palaver about *trample therapy* was just an excuse to vent her frustration at not being male.

Her *super persona* would be that part of her unconscious mind acting as a conscience and causing her to reject and revolt against the 'beast' I had become – rich, successful and maybe even ambitious for absolute power. Could that be a motive? Had this spurred her on to do the deed out of introjections whereby she had regressed to the values of her parents whose achievements were only mediocre? Was it the disappointment when she realised that I was not mediocre and quite the opposite. Or was it the primitive instinct of the *sotto ego* that prompted her to be rid of me and claim my demise as a trophy to possess forever? All were possible motives and her *persona analysis* ticked affirmative to all three possibilities.

Scupper's persona profile also suggested that he could well be a part of the puzzle. It showed he suffered from *castration anxiety* because he could never be me, which was the *ego ideal* of his conscious mind. He also had a personality complex of wanting to be something that he could never be, namely me. All three would be good enough reasons to want me out of the way so that he could assume my role and be totally independent of me at the same time.

Next, I needed to research the way the deed was carried out. I found a letter signed in my own name by my own hand, addressed '*To Whom It May Concern*' at The Alliance of the Heel of Achilles headquarters in Woccowaccaland. It expressed my grave concern that as president of Umbugumbuland I considered myself unfit to rule by being of unsound mind. I offered a substantial amount of money as a research grant to Mocknot Falls Psychiatric Hospital in return for a commitment that I would be admitted as a patient under the pseudonym of Wattle McBottle, never to be released, and that my admission under those terms and conditions remain confidential.

That whole sequence of events was totally foreign to me. Sure, I did seek help from Mocknot Falls Psychiatric Hospital, but I did it in person under a pseudonym and not by letter. No, I did not write or sign that letter and had no knowledge of it. Yes, the research grant was funded and paid from my account but not by me. I did not have a death wish, but someone else obviously did have one for me. Yes, I blame both Scupper and Blithe. Together they plotted to remove me. Blithe would have issued a legitimate certificate of unsound mind as my psychologist, and Scupper would have done all the left-brained stuff to carry it through.

Now that they had failed, I was obliged to banish them from my world. I was resolute that I would have nothing more to do with them.

That settled, I discovered that while Umbugumbuland's 'most wanted' was locked away at Mocknot Falls in Woccowaccaland, 'The Mob' was creating havoc back in Umbugumbuland.

'The Mob' was the group responsible for introducing some drastic changes in Umbugumbuland while I was away, and it seemed to materialise from nowhere. The whole thing was obviously a COIN job, but there was no evidence of any individual public servant as instigator. Instead, it was the public service itself that was 'The Mob'; a virtual army of COINs was in control. They had staged a military-style coup which was bloodless and advocated two major changes. The first was to introduce biometric data chips that would eventually ensure their authority could never be challenged. The second was to relieve the super-wealthy of all their wealth and bequeath it to the State.

Based on the technology of transponders, a data chip was inserted in a card or as a biochip implant inserted under the skin and no larger than a grain of wheat. The chip was a passive transponder with no battery or energy of its own. Known as an RFID chip, data was transported through radio frequencies via satellite.

Data stored on the transponder included the individual's fingerprints, footprints, eye scan, DNA genotype, financial status, medical history and personal history. Umbugumbuans could use the transponder either as a card or an implant to shop online or buy or sell anything pertaining to merchandise. They would be able to gain admission to any entertainment event, health club or hospital. They could travel on public buses, trains and aeroplanes simply by extending their implanted hand or flashing their card. They could communicate with their iPhone or home computer; lock, open and start their car without a key, and even keep track of their children going to school or at day care.

Decreed by The Mob, every citizen was expected to avail themselves of this gift of technology within ten years. Most people believed you'd have to be mad not to want to adopt the technology as it was free and The Mob had convinced the majority that the transponders provided the best protection against terrorists. Citizens who refused to conform were issued with a NUTS Certificate, which gave them access to public hospitals and public transport; and international travel if the need arose. However, at such times, they had to show ID and fill out a Form 666 to request a transfer to a COIN Certificate before being granted access to such services. As well, they were granted the added benefits of being exempt from paying tax and could do anything else they would have to be mad to want to do. The package had something for everyone, especially the needy, so in that sense the government was being true to AAA Party promises.

People were most excited about not having to get into checkout lines when shopping for groceries and the like as all items were automatically scanned and charged to their account and a receipt issued. Of course, it was bad news for shoplifters. However, there was one major problem that nobody was told about. Just as the transponder was turned on, it could also be turned off, which meant you could not buy or sell anything, go to a doctor, be admitted to hospital or use public transport. That was a real bummer and very sobering for people who wanted to stray from the path of righteousness.

An added benefit to the government was that biometric data chips could be used on people in the military who were all NUTS and were given no choice in the matter anyhow. The argument was that every soldier had a tracking device which could be used to keep them safe and differentiate friendlies from enemies. Even their vehicles were fitted with GPS technology.

Already the defence department was working on genetically enhanced cybernetic super-soldiers who were microchipped or had electrodes implanted in their bodies to control their internal organs and brain function. They also plied them with hallucinatory drugs to numb some of their normal tendencies like the need to fall asleep, the fear of death, and reluctance to kill.

The super-soldier pathway was particularly ideal for NUTS who were conscientious objectors. These people had their genetic code altered by modifying bits of DNA to create a new type of human specimen; one that functions like a machine, killing tirelessly for days and nights on end.

In case you might think all of this is an original idea, then I should acknowledge that it was all in the Bible – Revelation 13: 16–18. That's why I could not bring myself to do anything about it.

'And he causeth all, both small and great, rich and poor, free and bond, to receive a mark on their right hand, or in their foreheads: And that no man might buy or sell save he that had the mark, or the name of the beast, or the number of his name. Here is wisdom. Let him that hath understanding count the number of the beast: for it is the number of a man; and his number is six hundred three score and six.'

Good old triangular number 666. Go figure!

No doubt, the other measure regarding 'relieving the super-wealthy of their wealth' that The Mob adopted could only have been imagined by people who were totally out of their minds. Overnight, Unexplained Wealth Laws were passed to allow the government to seize, confiscate or sequester the private wealth of the super-rich until they could prove how they legally obtained their assets. This reversing of the burden of proof was draconian and insurmountable considering all records of financial transactions in Umbugumbuland had been seized and marked 'Not Accessible to the Public' quoting national security concerns that money was being paid to fund terrorist activities at home and abroad.

The new laws stated that 'any wealth or income that individuals cannot prove was legally acquired will become a debt payable by that person to the State'. They also required that such proof be tendered within one year from when the laws were passed and that 'time is of the essence'.

Historically, whenever problems arose that appeared so grossly unfair and downright ridiculous, people could take to the streets and demonstrate against the government. In this case, however, because wealth was defined by the laws as 'above a certain threshold', only the super-rich were affected. Since the number of super-rich was relatively small, and because they generally didn't have the balls for demonstrations, the media could offer no evidence of discontent. As there was no evidence of discontent, the rest of the world assumed everything was business as usual in Umbugumbuland. People kept streaming across our borders by plane, boat, and even rubber dinghies with all their cash, gold and diamonds, which were confiscated on arrival and frozen subject to scrutiny as possible 'unexplained wealth'. That eliminated the threat of any potential refugee problem.

You had to be mad not to realise that this was a Get Rich Quick scheme that the COINs, which was The Mob, thought up to rip off rich people. Anyhow, there wasn't much anyone could do because people seemed to love getting ripped off, especially at the hands of Get Rich Quick spruikers. It was a fact of life.

When I asked the average guy on the street, I found out people actually believed that the more money and assets the government sequestered, the more money there would be available for pensions to go up in the future. People were signing up in droves for COIN certificates and converting their NUTS certificates by filling out Form 666 and showing their ID so they could be eligible for the increased pension. The price of COIN certificates began to skyrocket just as I had predicted, and nobody either at home or abroad wanted to deal in anything but COIN certificates.

I decided there was nothing I could do to stop any of The Mob's initiatives; the latest being the newly printed COIN certificates with a picture of Aleph McNaught to the left of the watermark and below the Eye of Providence. Under my name I am also acknowledged as 'The Founder of Absurdism'. I would have to be mad to even contemplate complaining.

Scupper, the embodiment of my left brain, redeemed himself by leaving all his possessions to the State and becoming a farmer like his real father the great scholar who he'd never met. He bought back the original farm where his father and eccentric grandfather once lived. He demolished the mansion the previous owner had built on the cliff overlooking the sea. From a picture that his mother gave him, hidden until after Jack died, he arranged to have a crofter's hut built from stone, grass, bark and mud. They say he goes back there from time to time to sleep in it, and at night sometimes, he leaves a lamp on. Other than that, no-one has seen him.

Blithe, my right brain psychological mindset, repented and joined a sect led by a guru from Ellifafaland. He advised her to go on a retreat into the wilderness to rediscover herself. She never returned or she never left. It was one or the other. I'm not sure because sometimes she's here and sometimes she's not.

Yeahwellah, my shadow and religious mindset, has returned from the dead and has been stalking me lately. He keeps knocking on my door but when I open it, he's not there.

As for you, Thee, you've got better things to do and better books to read than read the crap in this diary.

I gave you the option way back to shut the book and go back to what you believed in before you met me. You're the one who decided to commit to this love affair with me and my beloved crippled country. If you find yourself stuck with a conscience or you have any regrets, you only have yourself to blame. That's the message.

Lol

Aleph. X

PS: Yeah … well …ah … well … I was gonna say. 'Just kidding'.

PPS: No, I'm not!

MORE FROM DAVIDE A. COTTONE

1965: *The Third Half.* Absurd Drama: (Eunice Hangar Lib, UQ).
1968: *Once Borrowed.* Novel (Fiction).
1978: *Bo.* Musical (Political Satire).
2001: *The Comeback Kid.* Musical (60's and 70's Rock) Performed H.K. 2001.
2002: *The Messenger.* Drama (Religious).
2002: *Generation Z: The Male Mutants.* Novel (Fiction). Pub: P.I.E Books.
2003: *Soul For Sale.* Musical (Contemporary). Performed H .K. 2003.
2005: *The Battle of the Sexes.* A Guide.
2006: *The Other World Album.* Songs (Seven songs by Sotto Ego).
2007: *Out of Control.* Musical (Rock, funk, soul, disco).
2009: *Eroica.* Musical (Classical).
2009: *Diary of a Devoted Poet.* "The Remembrance" Series. Pub: P.I.E.Books.
2012: *Canecutter.* Novel (Historical fiction). Pub: P.I.E.Books.
2012: *Il Calzolaio.* (The Shoemaker) Mystery Drama in English.
2014: *Sotto il sole australiano.* Novel (Fiction) in Italian. Pub: P.I.E.Books.
2014: *Portrait of a Devoted Poet.* "The Twilight" Series. Poetry. Pub: P.I.E. Books.
2015: *Vietnam … Viet-Bloody-Nam.* Novel (Historical fiction). Pub: P.I.E.Books.
2015: *Vietnam … Viet-Bloody-Nam.* One Act Play. Performed Brisbane. 2015.

Canecutter

Davide A. Cottone

A young Sicilian refuses to bow to the dictator Mussolini in the streets of Agira and is threatened with retribution by his Fascist thugs, the *Black Shirts*.

He hides in the mountains near his home town and arranges for a passport to Australia in 1924. Twelve years later, when he returns to Sicily to visit his family, he discovers Mussolini's dictatorial regime is not only entrenched but also unforgiving.

He could have had another life, instead he chose one of freedom as a canecutter in the fields of Far North Queensland.

This story is based on his life as a child and a fugitive in Sicily, as a canecutter, a farmer with a young family in a foreign land and as a classified *enemy alien*. His stoic belief in the innate goodness of his fellow human beings and his faith in God are put to the test time and time again in his valiant struggle against adversity and the harsh contrasts of Australian life.

Available at www.piebooks.net

Canecutter – Review

Professor Clive Moore: University of Queensland

Davide Cottone's *Canecutter* is an evocative account of the life journey of Sicilian immigrants to Babinda in North Queensland. The strength of the book revolves around surviving letters to and from Sicily, which provide the core of the narrative, and the sheer resilience of a family who survived many hardships. Carmelo died in 1985 and Elena in 1987, having created their own dynasty in North Queensland.

While *Canecutter* is centrally about Sicilian immigrants, it is also the story of many other similar families who carved small cane farms out of the virgin scrub and rainforest of the Queensland coast. Davide has written this historical novel of his father's life with literary flair, recording a by-gone era as settlement advanced in early twentieth century Queensland, when success was governed by physical strength to clear the land, and above all perseverance in the face of adversity. Carmelo Cottone was a quiet achiever, capable of confronting misguided authority, whether it be the internment officials or the Premier of Queensland, but essentially he was a family man who created a new life for both his immediate and extended family. *Canecutter* is also evocative of life in small North Queensland towns.

Davide Cottone has written a fitting tribute to his family. He has also advanced our understanding of the evolving sugar industry, from its days of human and horse labour through to mechanization, and of the lives of those who opened the north to agriculture and created a multi-racial society.

Professor Clive Moore, CSI, FAHA
Head of School
School of History, Philosophy, Religion and Classics
The University of Queensland